Sunset Behind Lavender Cottage
Emma Lewis

He tells me to jump. Behind me are snooty guys with their eyes on my new fortune. Below me is a handsome man who promises to catch me. What should I do?

Summoned to a funeral for a great-grandfather she'd never met, Rowan discovers she's now the juicy bait in a lake of men after her new fortune. She barely makes her rent each month and now she's the heiress to a large estate in England.

Adam never expects to be the hero of the day. But if he catches the girl, will it cost him his job? He works on the Mayfield estate, taking care of his dad's job until his dad is well enough to return, but what he'd really like to do is return home to Boston.

Rowan is given a choice by her new family. Marry someone they approve of or relinquish her inheritance. What if there's a third option? A fake boyfriend. A fake boyfriend who wants to go home, just like Rowan. Will Adam agree or is asking him to be the hero a second time too much?

Contents

Chapter 1

Rowan

"Rowan, you can't run away now."

The exasperated voice of my aunt followed me down the hall.

I wasn't running. I was just... leaving quickly. Minus my jacket and bag because I forgot them in my haste to get away.

I didn't slow even after the second, more exasperated call. Black-clad mourners scattered, startled looks on their faces, as I bolted toward them. Maybe they were afraid I'd bowl them over.

"Rowan Mayfield, come back!"

Nope, I was gone. Rowan Mayfield had left the building.

I'd done my duty and put up with the curious glances from the rest of the family, combined with the curl of their top lip once they discovered who I was, but now I'd had enough of the Mayfield clan, particularly the snooty British ones. I was leaving and they could all sneer without me having to watch.

I should have ignored that stupid letter from the lawyer. But it wasn't every day a thick cream envelope with 'urgent' written on the outside was jammed into my mailbox. Curiously, I had scanned the contents of the letter from Armstrong and Fox-William, then picked my jaw up off the floor.

I'd read it again. No way! I had been 'summoned' to my grandfather's funeral. He was my late mom's estranged father. I'd never met him and never thought I would. The letter made it clear that the family expected me, an outsider, to attend his funeral in England.

If it hadn't been for my mom, I'd have told them where to stick their summons. I should have told them. Not one of the Mayfields who'd just sneered at me had bothered to attend my mother's funeral.

"If I hadn't seen you in your coffin, I'd have killed you myself," I said under my breath as I dodged a small group of Armani black-suited middle-aged men.

Maybe not low enough from some of the outraged looks I received. I didn't care. The old coot had just managed to turn my life upside down and I'd never even met him.

Five minutes ago, I had discovered I was the major beneficiary of a multi-million-pound estate from my grandfather, and now everybody wanted to talk to me. Or kill me. I wasn't sure which. The gasp in the room as the family lawyer announced the decision had quickly turned to outraged babbling.

I stared at the lawyer, convinced I'd just heard him wrong. "What did you say?"

Mr. Fox-William fixed me with a hooded gaze. "You have inherited the entire Mayfield estate.

There are a few other beneficiaries, of course. And there are bequests to other members of the family."

"This is ridiculous," one of the men burst out. A cousin, I think. "Who is this girl? We don't know her. She could be any tart."

I turned to face him, and he flinched under my icy stare. Good. I may have gone from rags to riches in the space of a minute, but I could hold my head up high in front of these awful people. I wasn't sure what a tart was, but judging by his sneer, it wasn't good.

It was bad enough that I had to deal with the outrage from the rest of the family who were also strangers to me, but the second I left the study, desperate to get away from the anger directed at me, I was suddenly the focus of attention of everybody in the house.

One young man had his eyes fixed on me. He was just a little taller than my 5ft 8" with a weak jaw and predatory eyes. I saw him head toward me and made my escape, hurrying toward the open windows that led onto the balcony and down to the gardens. It was only when I reached the balcony, I realized I'd made a huge mistake. There were no stairs, just a wide stone balcony with seats and tables to look out over the view. I was trapped, nowhere to go, and he was bearing down on me, mouth open in a fake smile and pointy teeth bared.

I glanced over the thick stone railing. It wasn't a long drop to the path below, but I'd be lucky if I didn't twist an ankle. I looked back into the room.

The guy had the expression I'd seen on nature documentaries about sharks hunting their prey. I was suddenly a juicy steak.

My choice was angry people or the shark; I'd risk the ankle. I slipped my shoes off, stupid things anyway, and climbed onto the balcony railing.

"What the hell do you think you're doing?"

I straddled the wide railing and looked down at the sound of a man's voice, riddled with curiosity. His accent almost made me homesick. "You're from Boston?"

"I am." He grinned at me, his green eyes sparkling with amusement. "Why are you throwing yourself over the balcony? It can't be that bad."

I put him around thirty. Tall, broad-shouldered, a nice smile. He was tanned as if he spent a lot of time in the sun and I liked the faint fan of lines around his eyes. He wasn't dressed like the bespoke-suited and booted men in the room behind her. He was wearing flannel shirts and wranglers and had a big ugly hat on his head. A really ugly hat. I liked it. He was home to a girl who was a fish out of water.

"Trying to get away from sharks," I said, jabbing a thumb to indicate behind me.

His thick, dark eyebrows shot up comically. "Over the balcony?"

"There's only one way to go," I pointed out. "Are you going to catch me or laugh at me?"

"I can multi-task," he grinned, "but I'm covered in dirt."

Beggars, even ones in receipt of a huge fortune,

couldn't be choosers. "I don't care." The shark was almost upon me.

"Lily and Greg are never going to believe me when I tell them about this." He held out his arms. "Come on then, Ms. Boston-lady. Jump!"

It was now or never. I launched myself at the man and prayed he would catch me.

I landed in his arms. We both gasped and he held me tight against his wide chest as I flung my arms around his neck.

"Okay?" he asked.

"I am now." I realized I was still clinging to him and staring into his amazing eyes.

I let go of my stranglehold around his neck. I coughed and he started, as if he hadn't realized he was still holding me. He eased me to the ground. I winced as I trod on a small stone. I'd left my shoes back on the balcony.

"I need to get away from here," I muttered.

"Okay then, come with me."

I loved that he didn't ask me unnecessary questions. He just held out his hand. I took it because what was my alternative? Climb back to the balcony after throwing myself into his arms?

He raised an eyebrow. "Can you run?"

"800m running champ in junior high," I said.

He grinned and he bolted across the grass, one hand holding his hat. I ran after him, ignoring the startled cries above me. I was aware my companion was slowing his stride to match mine, but he didn't seem impatient, and I kept pace. The years of running finally paid off. I had no idea where he was leading me, but it didn't matter. If he led me away from the sharks, I was a happy girl.

As we pounded across the immaculate lawn it did occur to me that blind trust was how victims in horror novels and movies ended up in the hands of the bad guy.

"You're not a serial killer, are you?" I gasped.

He smirked at me. "Not today, sweetheart. I can't promise about tomorrow."

"I'll take today as a good sign. I plan to be a long way from here tomorrow."

His pace slowed and he jogged down towards a small hut. I could see the door was open although I couldn't see inside.

I followed him inside the shed, blinking as my eyes adjusted to the sudden darkness. "Is this my hidey hole?"

"Do you think anyone will come to look for you?" he asked.

"I've no idea," I admitted. "I've never been here before today and I don't know any of those people."

He gave me a curious look. "Why are you running away from them?"

I sighed and pushed my sweaty hair back from my face. "It all got a bit too much. One minute I was at my grandfather's wake and the next I'm heir to his fortune."

His eyes widened almost comically. "You're a Mayfield? You're one of the family?"

I shook my head. "I may be a Mayfield but I'm *not* one of them. My mother was a Mayfield, but she was estranged from her father. This is the first time I've been here."

He studied me for a long while and I started to get that predatory feeling again. Then he smiled and his green eyes twinkled. "I should have guessed from your eyes. You're a big improvement on the rest of them," he admitted. "Did you just say heir? You're kidding, right? You can't be the old man's heir?"

I grimaced. "If by the old man, you mean William Mayfield, then yes, the old coot just left me the whole estate."

He started to laugh. I watched him curiously, not sure why he found it so funny. He laughed until he clutched onto the small table behind him for support, and tears streamed down his face.

"Are you going to share the joke?" I snapped.

It took a few minutes for the guy to be able to speak. His chest heaved and he wiped his eyes. Then he shook his head. "You have no idea just how funny and absurd this whole situation is."

He laughed again but I failed to find the joke. "Don't you work for the Mayfield family?"

"I do," he agreed. "I'm the gardener."

"What's your name?"

"Adam Carless. From Boston as you guessed. At your service." He gave a bow and I started to feel I was the butt of the joke I didn't really understand.

"Nice to meet you, Adam," I lied. "I'm Rowan Mayfield."

"Good to meet you, Ms. Mayfield."

"Call me Rowan."

He pulled a wry smile. "That's not how they work here. You are family therefore you are Ms.

Mayfield, and I am Carless."

I stared at him open-mouthed. "Really? They do that *Downton Abbey* thing here?"

Adam shrugged. "You've met them, right? I'm just the gardener, it's the way it is."

"But that's ridiculous. This isn't some snobby country house in Jane Austen's England."

He outright laughed at my horrified expression. "Oh, Rowan, you are in for a huge culture shock. I can't wait you to really meet the family."

I eyed him curiously. "I always feel you're using the word family with a capital F."

Adam chuckled again. "That's how it feels."

"I'm not one of them," I said fiercely.

"Not at the moment. Not one of the Mayfields would run across the lawn barefoot to end up hiding in the gardener's shed."

"Are you going to get into trouble?"

The last thing I wanted was to cause trouble for Adam. I'd be gone in a few hours. He was stuck here.

He shrugged. "I don't know who you are. As far as I'm concerned, you're a guest of the house who wanted to do a tour around the gardens."

I eyed him skeptically. "Do you catch many shoeless guests in your arms and run with them away from everybody else?"

"I do whatever they tell me to do," he said easily.

"Why don't I believe you?"

"You can believe what you like," he said. "It's not a bad job if you can put up with the family.

They don't bother me much."

"How long have you been here?"

"Two and a half years. My parents moved here and I stayed in Boston. Then my Dad got sick and couldn't do his job. I said I'd take over until he is better. It's just taken longer than we expected.

"How's your dad?" I asked.

I regretted asking as soon as I saw the sadness in his eyes. "You don't have to answer that if you don't want to."

"It's okay." His sigh told me it was anything but okay. "He's not doing so well. Cancer. He might not be able to come back."

For some reason I leaned forward and patted his forearm. His tanned skin was warm under my palm. "I'm so sorry, Adam."

He forced a smile. "Thanks. At least I'm with him and can help my mom. She needs help to take care of him."

"Will you stay here?" I asked.

"I've been taking my time to decide." Adam admitted. "I live with Mom and Dad, so I don't have to pay rent. I don't want to settle in Boston only to turn around and have to come back. But I am homesick."

"My mom died three years ago," I said. "None of her family here bothered to come to the funeral. I sent them the details, but I heard nothing. I don't even know why I came."

I did know why. I wanted to look the people who'd ignored Mom and me in the eye and demand to know why. But my grandfather had dropped his bombshell first.

I saw the pity on his face now. "I'm so sorry, Rowan, no wonder you feel bitter toward them."

"That's just it. I feel nothing toward them at all," I admitted. "They're irrelevant to me. I'm going to go home and forget they ever existed."

"That's not really possible, dear."

I looked up at the light, feminine voice. A woman stood in the doorway. I took a moment to place her as one of my mother's half-sisters. Was it Willow or Ash? Willow, I think. The Mayfield girls all had tree names. I'd been lucky to end up with Rowan. My Gran had insisted on carrying on the tradition and called my mom Laurel even though William Mayfield had walked out on her.

Willow was probably in her late fifties, with light blonde hair set in a becoming bob. She wore a black suit which probably cost more than my entire wardrobe. Then again, I lived in old T-shirts and jeans.

Willow held out my shoes, jacket, and bag. "You left these behind."

I took them a little sheepishly. "Thanks, Aunt Willow."

"You need to come back to the house, Rowan," she said briskly. "We need to discuss your wedding."

Chapter 2

Adam

I thought Rowan was about to pass out as the color drained from her face. She swayed and I grabbed her by her shoulders, easing her down onto my seat before she collapsed.

I saw Willow Mayfield glare at me, but as she wasn't the one trying to help her new niece, I ignored her until I knew Rowan was settled and not liable to faint.

I was here because of my father and the last thing I wanted was my parents to be made homeless. But I also knew what the family was like. Ruthless to the core. Rowan would just be a minor irritant and easily dealt with. My loyalties at that moment were firmly with my new friend.

"Are you all right, Rowan?" I asked. "Here." I uncapped a bottle of water that I'd had on my potting table, and handed it to her, staying within reach in case she needed me.

"Thanks, Adam." Rowan's hands shook as she wrapped them around the bottle and took a long drink.

Rowan took a deep breath, then another, and gave me a wan smile. "I'm okay." Her smile faded as she focused on her aunt. "What are you talking about, Willow?"

I noticed she dropped the honorific. From the way Willow's eyes narrowed, so did she.

Willow pressed her lips together. "As you can imagine, the reading of the will was a surprise to the family. We had no idea Father had any plans to include you in the inheritance."

"So you knew I existed?" Rowan snapped.

Willow shrugged as if it were unimportant. "Yes, of course we did. Father told us from an early age that he had a child in Boston with some woman. But we didn't know he'd kept in touch."

"That 'woman' was my grandmother," Rowan said icily. "And as far as I'm aware he had no contact with his first family after he deserted her."

I saw Willow bristle. Oh yes. No fun to have your father's misdeeds rubbed in your face. Particularly when a fortune was at stake.

"But none of you cared enough to reach out to us," Rowan continued. "Especially when my mom was ill. She asked me to contact her father before she died. I did, but you ignored us."

"That was...unfortunate."

I saw Rowan clench her fists at Willow's sneering tone. I put my hand over Rowan's. She took a deep breath and gave me a tight smile, telling me she was okay.

"You think my mom's death was 'unfortunate'?"

Willow wasn't stupid. She realized she'd stepped over a line. "I'm sorry. Let me rephrase that. I know how hard it must have been for you. But William wasn't in good health then, and we felt it better if he didn't attempt to travel."

"You couldn't have come in his place?" I

demanded. "Or one of the others. There are enough of you."

"I'm sorry," she repeated with a scowl at me for interrupting. "You weren't family, dear."

I clenched my jaw at her dismissive tone. How dare she speak to Rowan like that. From the way the color flooded Rowan's cheeks, she was as angry as me, but when she spoke, her voice was controlled. Not calm, but icily controlled.

"But I *am* family, Willow, and Grandfather William has just said as much. You may not like the idea, but you're going to have to get used to it."

I stared at her in admiration. Rowan had just evened the score. I waited to see how Willow would respond.

"By blood, maybe," Willow acknowledged. "But it must be obvious, even to you, that you're not one of us."

And *boom*! Willow sent another shot across the bows.

Rowan sat back in her chair. "You're right. I'm certainly not one of you. I have morals."

I held back a grin. They may not be the same family, but they were the same blood. Rowan could certainly add the same edge to her voice that Willow and William could. But she wasn't as confident as she was portraying. I could feel the tremor in her small hand under mine.

Willow took a deep breath. "The family have decided since you're obviously incapable of running the estate—"

"Oh?"

"Rowan, be reasonable." Now Willow sounded exasperated. "You're just a receptionist. You have no idea what you're doing. The best thing you can do is get married to a suitable match."

Rowan stared at her, open-mouthed in horror. I probably didn't look much better. I knew the family lived in a different world to me, but you didn't just marry someone off five minutes after you met them.

"You can't tell me who to marry," Rowan snapped.

Willow stared at Rowan as if she were a bug. "Be reasonable, dear." Her tone dripped condescension. "This is the Mayfield estate. It's the largest and wealthiest estate in the south of England, and we've have property all over the world. You have no idea what you've just inherited."

"I thought my family would be there to help me," Rowan said sweetly.

"We *are* here to help you. That's why I'm here now." Willow said in a patronizing voice. "As we see it, you have two options. You marry someone this family chooses, or you renounce your inheritance. We'll pay you off with a small annual stipend."

And now the gloves were off. They knew Rowan would never marry a total stranger. What they really wanted was to be rid of her. This was a standard Mayfield tactic. Pay off the problem. Make it go away. I could feel the anger rolling off Rowan in waves. I leapt in before she went up in flames.

"Let me get this right, Ms. Mayfield." I made my tone as polite as I could. Normally Willow and I got on just fine, but she still expected me to acknowledge her status. Willow focused her laser gaze on me.

"Rowan is rightfully the heir of the Mayfield estate, but you want to marry her off to some distant cousin." I heard Rowan gasp. I really needed to tell her about the cousin thing over here. "Alternatively, you get her to sign her inheritance away. She goes home with a few dollars, and you all live happily ever after with her money."

Willow had gone crimson at my description but reluctantly she nodded. "We have an estate to maintain. I'm sure you can understand that. Rowan will be offered a suitable amount to invest. You can live comfortably, if you don't spend it all at once." She sniffed.

"Alternatively, you can go away," Rowan suggested. "I can pay you each a suitable amount to invest. You'll be able to live comfortably if you don't spend it all at once."

I snorted at the idea. I knew I was treading a fine line here. They were my employers, after all. But where did they get off treating Rowan like dirt beneath their feet.

Willow looked horrified. "I'm a Mayfield."

"So is she," I pointed out.

I remembered Greg's comment about his friend, Elle Ralston. There were Ralstons, and *Ralstons.* Well, Rowan had just become *the* Mayfield. And the rest of the Mayfields were scared their cushy lifestyle was about to come to an end.

"This is ridiculous," Willow snapped. "You know as well as I do how hard it is to run this estate, Carless."

"His name is Adam," Rowan said icily.

I squeezed her hand. "It's okay, Rowan."

"It really isn't," she muttered.

I liked this girl. She was going to shake things up around here.

Rowan fixed her gaze on Willow. "I'm going to make a decision about what I do. Not you. Not the family. You don't know me yet, but no one makes decisions for me."

Inwardly I was cheering. *You go girl!*

"You aren't making a choice between tea and coffee," Willow sneered. "The Mayfield Estate has been in our family for generations."

"I don't drink tea and I'm not about to pawn the house."

Willow actually shuddered at the thought. "Then you need to marry."

Rowan shook her head. "I'm sorry, I should have told you sooner. I'm already engaged."

I blinked. Rowan hadn't mentioned she had a boyfriend, let alone she was engaged. I felt a sharp pang of disappointment. I barely knew her, but anyone who would stand up to the Mayfield family was someone I would love to get to know.

Willow narrowed her eyes. "Oh? And who are you getting married to?"

Rowan smiled at her. "I'm marrying Adam."

Chapter 3

Rowan

When I got up this morning, I was Rowan Mayfield, a twenty-seven-year-old receptionist (among other jobs) living from paycheck to paycheck, who'd traveled halfway across the world to discover I was the heir to a wealthy estate in England. And now I'd just claimed the handsome gardener who caught me in his arms was my fake fiancé, to save me from a family who wanted to marry me off to a distant cousin (eww!), to get their hands on the money I'd only just found out I'd inherited. I think I'd gotten that right in my head.

Stop, world. I want to get off. At least until it quit throwing curveballs at me.

Adam was wide-eyed as he stared at me. Maybe I should have asked him first. He might already be married. I hadn't even considered that. This could all blow up in my face.

"Is that right?" Willow demanded.

Silently I pleaded with Adam not to ruin my story. He looked at me for a long time before he gave me the briefest of nods. He took my hand. It was warm and strong and for some reason it grounded me and stopped me flying away.

I smiled at Willow. "Willow, this is Adam, my

fiancé."

"Ridiculous," Willow snapped. "Carless is our temporary gardener. Er…"

"Adam." I smiled at him. "My fiancé's name is Adam."

Adam slipped his ugly hat off and I blinked. He was transformed from a sweet man trying to help me out, to something hotter, more…just more. He didn't let go of my hand.

"I met Rowan after her mom died," Adam said. "We kept in touch when I had to move over here. We joked that she could be related to the Mayfields but we had no idea it could be true." He looked so disingenuous I could almost believe his story.

"This is ridiculous," Willow muttered.

She should see it from my side.

I shifted closer to Adam. "I thought you'd be happy for me, Willow." I could do disingenuous too.

"You know that he's—" She stopped, obviously aware she was about to be rude about Adam to his face.

I opened my eyes as wide as I could make them. "Yes?"

"You need someone who's—"

"Yes?"

Her face pinched at my wholly fake innocent expression, but there's no way I was going to make it easy for her.

Adam nudged me. "Ms. Mayfield thinks I'm not good enough for you, sweetheart."

Willow looked down her nose at Adam. "You

need someone who isn't after your money."

"I didn't have any money until thirty minutes ago," I pointed out. "And he loved me then." I really hoped Adam wouldn't contradict me as I turned huge eyes on him, but the loving expression in his sparkling green eyes took my breath away. He deserved an Oscar for his acting skills.

Willow made a noise in the back of her throat. "Look, I know you must be disappointed, Carless—Adam," she amended hastily at my glare. "But even you can see we're in a difficult situation here. It would be better for all concerned if Rowan came back to the house with us and we discussed the best way forward as a family."

"Not without me." Adam's voice was so cold I turned to look at him. "You'll just try to bully her into signing away her inheritance. I'm coming with her, and we'll arrange a lawyer too."

"The Mayfield family have lawyers," Willow said.

"I know." He didn't sound impressed. "Rowan needs a break. She'll come back to the house later."

"But—"

"Later." He was unfailingly polite but when Willow stalked out of the shed, I turned to him.

"I am so sorry, Adam. I don't know what's gotten into me. I'll tell her the truth."

Adam gave me a wry smile. "You won't say anything to them. Not until you've gotten them tied up in knots."

I took in a shuddery breath. I had no idea what

to do next. "Aren't you worried about your job? I don't want you to be sacked just for helping me."

"I'm more worried about what they're gonna do to you," he said. "You don't know these people. The Mayfield family can be ruthless. Think what they're offering you. An impossible marriage or go home with a fraction of your inheritance."

"I don't care about the money," I said. That was the truth. I cared about making my rent and being able to eat. Beyond that it was all gravy, as my gran used to say.

"I know you don't," Adam said, still frowning. "But William Mayfield left you the estate for a reason. Don't throw it all away until you know why. Your aunts and uncles at least work for the Mayfield estate. There are cousins and other relatives who take, take, take. William never said no to them."

"I thought he was supposed to be ruthless," I said.

"He was an old man, sick, and he was lonely. Having the family around him made him feel better."

I studied him for a moment. "It sounds as if you knew him well."

"He spent a lot of time in the garden the last year. I listened to him talk about whatever was on his mind." Adam shrugged. "Not that any of the hangers-on would know that."

"You don't have much time for the family, do you?"

"The ones who work, yes. But this is a huge estate. If the others lifted a finger to help..."

The disgust in his voice was plain to hear.

"Okay." I took a deep breath. "I'll wait to see what they have to offer me, before I make any decisions."

"And don't do anything without talking to a lawyer."

I grimaced. "I don't have a lawyer. I've never been able to afford one."

Adam pulled out his phone. "I may be able to help there." He scrolled through his contacts, then he waited. "Greg? What time? Sorry, I didn't think. Listen, I need your help. Well, not you but Lily, and possibly your friend, Elsa."

That was the second time I'd heard him talk about Greg and Lily. Who were these people? And who was Elsa?

"The Mayfields. You've heard of them? Oh hi, Lily. Yeah, the Mayfields. Wait, let me put you on speaker too, it'll be easier."

"Greg, Lily, meet my friend, Rowan. She's just inherited the Mayfield estate. Rowan, meet my friend, Greg Crenshaw, and his wife, Lily. Lily was a Duchamp."

I stared at him. Lily Duchamp. Even I'd seen pictures of Lily Duchamp in the media. One of the wealthiest women in Boston and heir to the Duchamp Industries.

"Hi Rowan." Lily had a sweet voice. She also sounded like home which made me suddenly long to be back in my apartment surrounded by people who spoke like me.

"Hi, Lily," I managed.

"Hi Rowan, you sound like a local girl," Greg

said. "What are you doing with Adam?"

"Rowan is a Bostonian. Who's just became heir to the Mayfield fortune in England. Yeah, *that* Mayfield. But she's never met any of them before and she needs help. The family are putting pressure on her to marry or give up her inheritance."

"What she needs is a good lawyer," Greg said.

"She does." Lily hummed. "I'll call Elle now. She'll know the right person to talk to. Rowan, don't make any decisions until you've heard from me or Elle. If you need us, we can be on the next plane over."

"That's really kind of you." I couldn't get over how these people were willing to help a total stranger.

"Don't let them pressure you," she said.

"Thanks Lily," Adam said. "I'm going to stay with Rowan." He grinned. "I'm her fake fiancé."

I heard Greg snort at the other end of the line. "Her fake fiancé. Why does that not surprise me? We'll be back soon."

"I can't afford to pay for a lawyer," I admitted. "Not yet. I don't have any money."

"Don't worry about that," Lily said. "That's the least of your worries. Elle's just answered. Later. Yeah, hi lovely, we need your help."

"Call you soon," Greg said and then they were gone, and Adam and I were left staring at each other.

"What just happened there?" I asked, my head whirling.

Adam grinned. "You know who Lily is?"

I nodded. You couldn't live in Boston and not know Lily Duchamp.

"Lily's best friend is Elsa Ralston."

"*The* Elsa Ralston?" I asked, feeling faint.

These were women I'd only read about.

Adam nodded. "Well, buttercup, you've just joined their ranks. You'll be one of the richest women on the east coast. At least you will if you can hang onto your inheritance. But first you need help."

I saw a flaw in his plan. "But we're in England and they know American lawyers."

"One step at a time. First we get you lawyered up back home, and they can liaise with solicitors over here. I need to get changed. If I'm going to be by your side, I need something less...um...dirty."

I nodded. That was one thing I agreed with. Adam was covered in dirt from head to foot.

"Time to meet Mom and Dad. I can't wait to give them the news." He smirked at me. "You get a fortune, a fake fiancé, wealthy friends, and get to meet the parents in the same hour. You've had a busy day, Ms. Mayfield."

Chapter 4

Adam

The look of horror on Rowan's face would have been funny, except if I'd been in her position I'd have been curled up in a ball in the corner. She needed a friend until her brain kicked back online and I could be that friend, or fake fiancé. Whatever was needed.

Having Greg and Lily in my corner was a plus point. I couldn't think of two people better able to help a brand-new Bostonian heiress. I was just the gardener.

I looked down at her shoes. "You should put those on. At least until we get to my car."

Rowan grimaced but she slipped on the black shoes, and I led her out of the shed. I half expected Willow or one of the hangers-on to leap out behind the jasmine that was planted behind the door, but thankfully it was free of the family, and I guided her safely to my old Honda.

The car belonged to my dad, and he insisted I clean it every Saturday, so at least Rowan didn't have to worry about getting her black suit dirty. She didn't seem to care, sinking into the seat and closing her eyes.

"Tired?" I asked as I slipped behind the wheel.

"Exhausted," she murmured. "I think my

adrenaline is crashing."

"Jetlag and stress are not a good combo. You need coffee and to put your feet up for a while."

Rowan smiled. "You sound like my mom."

"I sound like *my* mom," I said ruefully as I drove toward the gate. "Our cottage is on the other side of the estate. It's quicker to drive around it, than through it."

I turned into the leafy country lane and headed toward the gate nearest the estate workers' cottages.

"How big is it?"

"This estate is just over twenty thousand acres. It's one of the biggest privately owned homes in the UK. They own others in the north of England, Scotland, and abroad. The Mayfields have always resisted opening the house and gardens to the public. The family has always been wealthy with diverse business interests, so they've managed to stave off that decision."

"Has my grandfather always lived here?"

I glanced at her. "You don't know much about your family history?"

"They're not my family and I don't know anything about them," she said. "My mom refused to talk about the Mayfields. She was so angry at how they'd rejected her mom. I mean, I knew I had rich relatives, but I was born on the wrong side of the tracks. I've never had time to investigate my family history. Too busy trying to make rent."

"I hear you," I agreed. "Well, Charles Mayfield bought this house in 1689. The Mayfield family were wealthy landowners before they arrived. We don't probe too deeply into how they made their money but they arrived in Boston in 1825. The two families have been interconnected since then. William went to school over there."

"Which was where he met my grandmother."

"Yes. I don't need to tell you what happened after that." I bit my lip, wondering whether to tell her what William had told me. "I think William always regretted leaving your grandmother behind."

"Penniless and pregnant, you mean?" Rowan sounded more amused than angry, but it had to hurt.

"Yeah. He didn't come out of it shining in glory, did he?"

"He destroyed her," Rowan said. "She was never strong and Mom worked three jobs to keep the family together and took care of her."

I decided not to relay William's regrets. What would a rich man's words mean to a family struggling to feed themselves?

"You liked him, didn't you?" Rowan said suddenly. "William. You liked him."

"I think it's more that I felt sorry for him," I said. "He was lonely, you know? So many people here and very few of them gave him the time of day except to ask for more money."

Rowan grunted. I didn't push it.

We drove back onto the estate, and I headed to the cottage at the end of the row where my parents lived. It was a tiny two-bed cottage. Since my dad had gotten sick, he slept downstairs. I took the small bedroom and my mom, the other. She kept talking about Dad getting better and moving back upstairs. We all knew it wasn't going to happen, but Dad and I never contradicted her. She needed that hope.

Rowan got out of the car and looked at the cottage with roses and clematis over the door. Her smile was wistful. "My mom always wanted to live in a home like this. She'd find pictures online and say that was her next home."

"My mom wants to go back to Boston and an apartment. She says the stairs are too much for her knees. She's only fifty-five so I think she might be exaggerating."

"We can do a swap," Rowan said.

We grinned at each other. She'd just inherited one of the largest estates in England. I didn't think a cottage, or a small apartment was in her near future.

I led her into the tiny front yard. My dad kept reminding me to call it a garden. Until he'd gotten sick, he'd maintained most of the gardens in the row of cottages. I'd taken over for him, knowing it gave him pleasure to look out of the windows at the blooming roses.

I opened the front door. "Mom, I've got a visitor. You'd better not be kissing Dad."

I heard Rowan's amused snort and grinned. I looked over my shoulder. "You think I'm joking. There's a reason I give a warning."

My mom and dad's love for each other hadn't dimmed in thirty-five years and that was all I was going to say.

"A visitor?" Mom came out, drying her hands on a towel, her eyes sparkling with curiosity.

"Mom, this is Rowan Mayfield, my fiancée. Rowan, this is my mom, Allyson Carless."

Both women gaped at me.

Mom gasped. "Your fiancée?"

"What on earth?" Rowan's eyes were almost comically wide.

I shrugged. "You were the one who decided we were engaged. You think I could have said it better?"

Mom shook her head and turned to Rowan. "You look exhausted, dear. Come into the kitchen and I'll put the kettle on. Then you can explain what my son is talking about."

"Dad?" I asked.

"He's asleep. He's had a bad morning."

I nodded, not needing an additional explanation. I led Rowan into the kitchen and pointed at the kitchen table. "Take a seat. I'm going to check on Dad, then have a quick shower and change. Mom, Rowan is William's granddaughter. She's just inherited the lot. The family are going to play nasty. I won't let that happen."

My mom pressed her lips together. "I understand. But I'm still not sure how you acquired a fiancée when you didn't have a girlfriend this morning."

"You should ask Rowan."

Mom cocked her head. "You're from Boston."

I saw Rowan blink rapidly and knew tears weren't far away. "Make her a coffee and treat her gently. It's been a stressful day for Rowan. I'll be back in five minutes."

As I walked out the door, I heard Mom say, "I'll put a pot on and you can relax for a moment, dear. You look like you haven't slept in days."

"Thank you, Mrs. Carless."

"Allyson, please. And Simon is the one lazing in bed. I'll introduce you another time."

I grinned. Rowan would be fine. I poked my head into what was now Dad's bedroom. He was in a hospital bed which took up most of the space. He was also snoring loud enough to wake the dead. I grimaced, backing out quietly and headed up the stairs.

My bedroom could just about take a queen-sized bed and a tiny closet. I missed my California king from home. But I didn't spend much time in here. I was either working in the gardens or spending time with my dad. I'd be going home soon enough. I would miss working in a garden like Mayfield, but I'd miss my Dad more.

I showered and changed into dark jeans and a dress shirt. Then I headed downstairs, just in time to hear my mom say, "So how did you meet my son?" I waited to hear Rowan's reply.

She didn't disappoint. "I threw myself over the balcony and into his arms about an hour ago. I...uh...needed a fiancée and your son was there. He...uh...didn't say no."

"Whirlwind romance, then," my mother said dryly.

"He saved me from the sharks."

"My son has his uses."

I snorted and walked into the kitchen. They both turned to look at me.

I grinned at Mom. "So now you know how I went from zero to hero."

She shook her head. "No one is going to believe this."

I sat down next to Rowan and squeezed her hand. "Until Rowan gets legal advice, they have to believe she and I are engaged."

"I don't think anyone will believe we're engaged," Rowan said.

"Maybe not, but if it means they give you a breathing space until they come up with their next nefarious plan, then I'm your loving fiancée. All we need is two socialites, a lawyer, and a cunning plan to fool them."

Rowan turned to my mom. "Is he always like this?"

"Usually he's worse. Who are the socialites?"

"Lily and Elle Ralston. I phoned Greg for help. Rowan needs a lawyer."

"Certainly more than she needs a fake fiancée," my mom muttered.

I frowned, not sure where Mom was going with this. I thought she'd find it as funny as I did. "You did get the fake part, yes? They want to marry her off."

I needed coffee to carry on this conversation. I waved the coffee pot at Rowan who shook her head. "Mom?"

"I'm fine." Mom huffed and sat back in her seat. "Rowan, you seem like a nice girl, but I'm not sure Adam getting involved is a good idea. We work on the Mayfield estate, and our home comes with the job. If they fire Adam, we'll have to find a new home. I don't think Simon is strong enough to cope with moving."

I think it was the first time my mom had admitted that things were bad with my dad. I suddenly realized that I'd not only put my job in danger, but their home too.

Rowan took her hand. "Allyson, whatever happens, Adam won't be fired."

"You can't know that."

"I'm a Mayfield. At the moment, I'm *the* Mayfield. Your home is safe."

I took a deep breath. Maybe there was more of William in her than she thought. I knew she'd keep her promise.

Before I could say anything, my phone buzzed. It was a local number I didn't recognize.

"Hello."

"Mr. Carless?"

At a guess an older man, sounding crisp and efficient. I didn't recognize his voice.

"That's right."

"My name is Jonathan Roberts. I'm a solicitor based in Lower Headley. I received a call from a colleague in Boston. I understand your friend is in need of legal advice."

I mouthed, "Lawyer," to Rowan, seeing the apprehension flood her. "Mr. Roberts. Thanks for calling. Tell me, are you connected to the Mayfield estate in any way?"

"No, I can assure you I'm not. I have undertaken work for the Ralston family in the past."

I breathed a sigh of relief. "Okay, I'm going to hand you over to my fiancée, Rowan Mayfield. She's the one who needs your advice."

I held the phone out to Rowan. "Jonathan Roberts. Lawyer. He's worked with the Ralstons, but he's not connected to your family."

She looked momentarily overwhelmed, but she took the phone.

"Mom and I are going to sit in the back yard. You stay here and take the call."

As much as I'd muscled in on her business, or was it the other way around, I didn't want Rowan to think I was controlling her.

I hustled Mom outside and we sat on the bench, basking in the early afternoon sunshine.

"What have you gotten yourself involved in, Adam?" Mom asked, her brow furrowed.

I shook my head. "I don't know, Mom, but I couldn't let Rowan be eaten alive by that family. They don't deserve her."

"Be careful, Adam. She could turn your life upside down."

"I think she already has," I said honestly as I pulled out my phone. "I need to call Charlie, to let him know why I'm AWOL this afternoon.

Charlie was the estate manager and my boss, and the biggest gossip around. I'd be surprised if the news hadn't already gotten back to him.

"So you're a married man, Prince Charming," he barked. "Do I need to call you sir and tug my forelock?"

"Who told you? What's a forelock?"

"Who didn't tell me. Janie from Accounts. Bill from the kitchen. Carol from...I can't remember where she's from."

"Stewards," I supplied. "She's working the funeral today."

"Course she is. Then I find my gardener is engaged. To the mystery American woman who's now the big cheese. Which is really strange because as far as I was aware, he was young, free, and single when he arrived for work this morning. Also he was working today and now he's not."

I caught the edge to his voice. I was going to have to smooth ruffled feathers here.

"I'm sorry, Charlie. I promise I'll make up the hours this week. Rowan and I were a thing before I came here. She didn't know the family before today. She's had a shock and I want to take care of her."

"I know you'll make up the hours, but you could have told me your girlfriend was coming over. I wouldn't have tried to set you up with my sister."

Funny you should say that.

Chapter 5

Rowan

I disconnected the call from Mr. Roberts and rested my head in my arms. I burst into tears. This whole situation was impossible. I just couldn't take any more. I wanted to get the next flight home and forget about the family and a fake fiancé. I wanted my little apartment and my two jobs. That was all familiar to me.

"Hey."

A warm hand rubbed soothing circles on my back. It was warm and familiar, and as much as I wanted to be left alone, it felt good too.

When I eventually managed to stop crying, I raised my head. Adam offered me a tissue.

"Thanks," I sniffled.

I wiped my eyes and blew my nose. "Sorry."

"Nothing to be sorry for. You've had an awful day."

He was right there.

"The lawyer wants to meet me this afternoon before I go back to the house. Could you call me a car?"

Adam chuckled. "This isn't like Boston. It's the middle of the countryside. You won't find an Uber on every corner. I'll drive you to the solicitor. I know where it is."

"What about your job?" I asked, worried I was going to make this worse for him.

He gave me a conspiratorial grin. "The boss asked me to drive her around this afternoon."

I managed a weak smile. "She did, huh? In which case, she needs to use the bathroom and find out if she looks like a panda." I blushed at Adam's careful look. "I have panda eyes, don't I?"

Adam squeezed my shoulder. "A bit. Go clean up and I'll let Mom know what we're doing."

"Where's the bathroom?"

"Through there." He pointed to a door off the kitchen.

I went into the bathroom and looked at myself in the mirror. The man had been generous. Panda eyes and red cheeks and nose. I wasn't a pretty crier. I jumped at the knock at the door.

"Yes?"

"Mom says there's a pack of make-up remover wipes in the cabinet under the sink."

"Thanks," I said huskily, and really, I wanted to cry again at the kindness.

I looked in the cabinet and found the packet of wipes. I tried to wipe away the tears but the make-up I'd carefully applied that morning was beyond saving. I wiped it all away and washed my face. I thought about reapplying it, but my eyes were too sore. Maybe later.

When I emerged from the bathroom, Adam was talking to his mom. He smiled at me as I approached.

"Feeling better?"

I nodded and smiled shyly at Allyson. "Thanks

for the wipes."

She patted my hand. "You're welcome. You go give the Mayfields what for."

"I don't want to cause you any trouble," I assured her.

Allyson waved her hand. "As my son rightly pointed out, it wouldn't be the right thing to do to leave you to that pack of wolves."

"Let's go," Adam said.

We headed for the car. There was a brief moment of confusion as I forgot the driver's side was on the right. Adam waited for me to orientate myself.

"One day I'm going to get this right," I muttered as I walked around the hood of the Honda.

"Don't worry, it took me months to get it right," Adam said. "The boys in the office had a bet when I'd finally go to the right side."

"They bet on something like that?"

Adam chuckled. "This lot would bet on how many hashbrowns are served at breakfast."

I shook my head. Men were strange.

Once again, we were driving out of the estate. I couldn't help the sigh of relief that escaped me when we passed through the wrought iron gates.

Adam grinned at me. "Glad to be out of there?"

"I don't belong there," I said with feeling.

"Not yet, you don't," he agreed, "but remember this is supposed to be all yours now."

I pressed my lips together and looked out of the window. I'd been trying to forget that.

He patted my knee. "Just relax and enjoy the

countryside. It's very pretty around here."

"It's nothing like Boston." I longed to be back with my familiar buildings and streets.

"No, it's not. But I like the open spaces."

"How did you end up being a gardener?" I asked.

"No money for school. I couldn't face all the debt. My dad had been a gardener all his life and I used to help him. I took over his business when he moved here."

"Why the estate?"

"Dad was born on the estate and wanted to retire here. Mom wasn't so keen, but she agreed for Dad's sake. He got a job as a gardener, and they've stayed here ever since. Then Dad got the cancer diagnosis, and I hated being so far from him. I had dual nationality thanks to Dad, so I sold my business, came over, and temporarily took his job."

"What will you do when he's better?" I asked.

He gave me a quick smile, but it was full of pain. "That's kind of you but short of a miracle, Dad isn't going to get better. The cottage and the job will go. I want to go home to Boston. Make a home for Mom and me until we're both settled. Dad made me promise to take care of her."

I didn't know what to say. Here I was grumbling about inheriting a country estate and Adam faced the loss of his father. It made me feel ashamed. I needed to stop relying on other people to solve my problems. I may just be a receptionist, but I was a darn good one. I needed to apply that to the rest of my life.

I looked at Adam and saw the pinched lines of his face. "If there's anything I can do to help, just let me know, okay?"

"Thanks." Adam sighed. "Let's deal with one problem at a time. First, the Mayfields."

"I hope this lawyer knows what he's doing," I muttered. "One of us needs to understand this mess."

It turned out that Mr. Jonathan Roberts knew what he was doing much better than a jetlagged receptionist. I don't know how but he'd already gotten hold of a copy of the will and had studied it before we arrived.

Mr. Roberts was younger than I expected. Maybe early forties. He had dark blond hair, ice-blue eyes behind thin-rimmed glasses, and the figure of a linebacker. I'd begged Adam to come into the meeting with me knowing I was too tired to think straight. He shook our hands and offered us coffee. I said yes because I needed the caffeine.

When hot fragrant coffee was in front of me, he said, "The good news is Mr. Mayfield was of sound mind when he made the will. The family solicitor is a friend of mine."

I stiffened and he obviously noticed. "I am not retained by any of the Mayfields, I assure you. Your affairs will be well handled by me."

I felt Adam brush my leg which I took to mean stay calm. "You said good news. What's the bad news?"

"The family is determined to contest the will, and they could win. Or tie you up in legal proceedings for years until you lose the will and money to fight them."

"How will that help them?" Adam demanded.

"It won't," Mr. Roberts agreed, "and I hope they will realize that once clear heads prevail."

But his dry tone suggested he didn't hold out much hope.

"I don't have a cent to my name. It'll be a short fight," I said. "They suggested I marry someone suitable." I didn't need the air quotes this time.

"Hence your sudden engagement," Mr. Roberts murmured.

"They only want me to marry so they can control the estate."

Mr. Roberts nodded. "It seems likely."

"They also suggested paying me off with a lump sum I could invest."

"Yes. I expected that from them."

Then Mr. Roberts fixed his eyes on me. He had the lightest eyes I'd ever seen. "What do you want, Ms. Mayfield?"

"Right this minute I want to go home. Ask me in the morning when I've had some sleep.

He nodded. "You need to think very carefully about what you want to do. Mayfield Estate is magnificent because it's been well taken care of by its owners."

I bristled because who was he to imply I wouldn't take care of it? Then a thought occurred to me. "Who do you think will take charge of the estate if they buy me out?"

"Willow, maybe. Harry doesn't want it. Ash and Raymond are too busy," Adam said, and Mr.

Roberts murmured his agreement.

"Then I might be as good as any of them?"

Mr. Roberts inclined his head. "That's a possibility."

I leaned back in my seat. "Then how do I change the family's mind and stop them draining the estate just to be—?" I cut myself off, suddenly remembering where I was.

"That is more difficult. Leave it with me. I'll make some inquiries. If your relatives press you, say you're considering all your options. I would suggest not returning to the house unless you have Mr. Carless with you."

Not by a word or a look did he suggest he knew our relationship was fake.

"I can't hide from them forever," I muttered.

Adam reached over and held my hand. "You don't have to, Rowan. We'll return tomorrow together."

"Where are you sleeping?" Mr. Roberts asked.

"I booked into a hotel. The Old Drake."

"I know it," Adam said.

That had been the one sensible move I'd made, even if it had cost me three extra shifts at the bar to help pay for it. I'd only booked for three nights though, and this was night two. I wasn't sure what to do after tomorrow night.

"Another thing I would suggest. Meet the staff on the estate. You can't make a decision on whether you want to stay without getting to know the place." Mr. Roberts's lips twitched. "You've already met the gardener. Find out their suggestions. You'll learn more about the workings of the estate from talking to the staff than you will taking cocktails in the drawing room."

I narrowed my eyes. "It sounds like you're speaking from experience."

"I was born at Farnham House nearby. My father was the estate manager. You'd be surprised how much he knew."

I turned at Adam's snort.

He grinned and shrugged. "Charlie's the biggest gossip in the county. Who do you think takes the bets?"

I made a decision. "I think tomorrow you and I should go on a tour of the estate."

Adam beamed at me. "I think that's a great idea."

I glanced at Mr. Roberts. "I'll leave my number. You can call me when you've made your...inquiries."

"I suggest you tell your relatives to funnel all inquiries regarding the will via me. You'll sort out the serious ones from the chancers."

A thought occurred to me. "Will the estate pay for all their legal bills?"

Mr. Roberts coughed. "I'm afraid I took the liberty of telling Mr. Fox-William that you would not allow any legal matters regarding the will to be covered by the estate."

In other words, if they wanted a fight, we'd give them one. I gave him a broad smile. "Thank you, Mr. Roberts."

Then another, less happy, matter struck me. If I cut the family off over the will, what about me? "Your bill—"

"This is being covered by Ms. Elsa Ralston and Ms. Lily Duchamp until your accounts are open."

My jaw dropped. Two women I'd never met were paying my legal bills?

"I'm sure you'll be in a position to pay them back when this is settled," he assured me.

"I hope so or I'll be washing their dishes for a long time," I muttered.

Adam grinned at me. "Ready to go?"

Almost in a daze, I shook hands again and Adam steered me to the car.

"What do I do now?" I asked him over the roof of the Honda.

He beamed at me. "Dinner?"

Chapter 6

Adam

From the lack of conversation, I could tell Rowan was flagging as I drove to a local pub for dinner.

I turned to her when I pulled into the parking lot at the side of the pub. "I know you're tired and you probably just want to crash." At Rowan's nod, I said, "But you need to eat, and the Crown do a good burger and fries. They do a salad too," I added hastily in case she thought I was making a comment about her weight. From the way her eyes widened I realized I was just digging myself a deeper hole. "I'm gonna get out of the car now, because whatever I say next is gonna be wrong."

She gave me a tired grin. "Burger and fries sound perfect."

I led her into the pub and waved at a couple of men from the estate I recognized. Their eyes widened when they saw who was with me.

"Rowan, are you up to being the big cheese now? Because those two guys work in Stewards, and they recognize you."

She straightened her back and nodded, forcing a smile on her face. "I can do that."

I led her over. "Rowan, this is Barry, and the big guy is Alfie. They work in Stewards."

Her smile became more genuine as she shook both their hands. "I remember. You guys were responsible for organizing the guest seating at the funeral."

Barry, a short, burly guy in his mid-thirties, made a derisive noise in the back of his throat. "It would have been easier to herd cats." His companion nudged him, and he added hastily, "Sorry, miss."

"Call me Rowan. It's okay. My mom used to say the same thing when she worked at a wedding venue. You did a great job, guys."

I wanted to chuckle as they preened at the praise from the pretty girl. But Rowan was doing fine without me. She asked them how long they'd worked at the estate and listened to Alfie's tale of being born there. It made me realize William may have been a lousy grandfather, but he had been a good employer. People stayed on the estate for life.

Eventually she turned to me and said, "You promised me burger and fries?"

"You got it. See you tomorrow, guys."

She shook their hands again, said she'd find them tomorrow, and followed me to the bar. Barry and Alfie didn't take their gaze away from her.

"Well done," I said, when we reached the bar and I'd greeted the bartender. I knew him from catered events at the estate. I introduced Rowan and they talked for a couple of minutes.

"Do you trust me to order for you?" I asked.

Rowan nodded. "Could I have a soda though. I

don't drink liquor."

I ordered the drinks and food. We had a quick tussle over who paid the bill, which I won. Rowan was too tired to put up a real fight. Then I led her to the Snug, which was a little corner of the pub tucked away from the bar area.

As we sat down, I said, "You just have to do that with a couple of hundred estate staff and you'll have them eating out of your hand."

"Barry and Alfie seem like nice guys," she said.

"They are," I agreed. "They're also quick to let you know if they don't like you. Some of the family have never said hello to them, shaken their hand, or gotten to know them like you just did. Respect goes a long way."

"I work in an office as the receptionist. I take extra shifts at a bar to make rent. I'm one of them," she pointed out.

"That will probably gain you more respect than anything else."

"Don't I have to be good enough to be part of the family?"

"You are," I said immediately.

Rowan smiled at me. "You know just what to say to make me feel better." She sighed and slumped back against the seat. "I'm going to need to find somewhere to sleep after tomorrow night. I can't afford to stay at the hotel. I understand I've just inherited this huge house."

I grimaced. "I can understand why you don't want to move in there, at least not yet. I'd invite you to stay with us but there's no room as Dad is downstairs. I'll talk to Charlie, the estate manager.

There might be an unoccupied cottage." I eyed her speculatively. "You could demand to stay at the house."

She shuddered. "You want to throw me in with the sharks? No thanks."

"Most of them don't live there. Only Willow, Harry, Ash, and Raymond have apartments at the house. William occupied the main rooms."

"I know Willow is my aunt. Who are the others?"

"Aunts and uncles. William married three times. His third wife, Wendy, died last year. Harry, her son, is a decent guy. He used to take care of William. He's a bit lost now. Not sure what to do with himself. You should get to know him." I made a mental note to introduce her to Harry.

She furrowed her brow. "Was he the one who gave the eulogy?"

"I wasn't there," I reminded her.

"Slim, tall, balding? A soft voice."

"That's him. He takes after his mother."

The food arrived and we stopped talking about the family. Rowan ate with an enthusiasm that pleased me. I couldn't be doing with people who picked at their food. We didn't bother talking until she sat back with a satisfied sigh.

"I needed that," she admitted.

"When was the last time you ate?"

The fact she had to think about it told me everything I needed to know.

"Yesterday I think," she said.

"Did you have breakfast this morning?"

Rowan shook her head. "I was too nervous to

eat or sleep."

"Make sure you eat tomorrow morning," I advised. "It's going to be a long day. The estate is huge. And wear proper shoes."

She grimaced. "I will. I don't think my feet could take another day in these torture devices."

I smirked. She'd kicked them off as soon as we sat down. "What made you buy them?"

"I needed something for the funeral. I usually live in sneakers and Converses. Doc Martens in winter."

"Do you wear them in the office?"

"I have a pair of flat black pumps for walking about the office. Most of the time people can't see my feet. My boss is the best. If I don't go barefoot in the office or in front of clients, she's cool."

"I can't wait for you to meet Elsa Ralston and her husband. You'd fit right in with them. They live in working boots."

"How did you become friends with the Boston elite?" she asked.

"Gardening," I explained. "I haven't actually met Lily in person, but I talk to her when Greg and I chat. She's very sweet. I met Greg through the business, and he took over some of my clients when I had to come here. Then he fell in love with Lily who was friends with Elsa. Elsa was a landscape gardener and had to sell her business when she inherited the family empire. Her husband owns a farm and animal sanctuary in Texas, so Elsa spends most of her time there. I'm also into art and Greg's grandmother is Marisa Ralston."

Rowan wrinkled her nose. "The artist?"

I nodded. "Greg took me to meet her a few times. She's wonderful. A total sweetheart. I call her once a month."

"I don't know much about art," she admitted, "and I've never met anyone famous."

I stretched out in my seat. "If you inherit the estate, you'll be the one who's famous."

Another grimace. I told myself to rein it in. I didn't want Rowan to think I was pressuring her in any way. She'd get enough of that from the family in the coming days.

"I'm just me, you know? Rowan Mayfield," she said. "It was always just Mom and me."

"I understand," I said gently. "Suddenly your world is so much bigger, and it's scary."

"If you hadn't adopted me, I'd probably have been on the first flight home."

"I'm glad you're taking time to get to know the place and its people. I love Boston. I miss it like crazy. But I never thought I'd get the chance to work in another country."

She frowned. "I'll need to sort out visas if I stay."

"One issue at a time," I suggested.

Rowan pulled a small, black notebook out of her bag and scribbled one word on a blank page.

Visa

She gave me a sheepish grin. "I write things down or I'll never remember them."

"Good idea," I agreed. "I make notes and photos on my phone. Charlie insists we photograph everything."

Rowan yawned suddenly, clapping her hand over her mouth. "I'm so sorry."

I drained the last of my Coke and put down the glass. "I'll take you to the hotel."

It was barely eight o'clock, but Rowan was working on fumes.

I waved at Alfie and Barry, then headed for the door. To my surprise, Rowan veered over to them again.

"It was good to meet you both," she said. "It must have been a hard day for both of you."

They looked surprised, but they nodded.

"I'm going to miss old Will," Alfie said. "He was always good to my old mum. She was ill a lot when we were kids and he let me and my sister play in the house to give her a break."

We said goodbye again and headed for the car. I couldn't help wondering if Rowan was angry at her grandfather showing his kindness to everyone except her family.

"They appreciate it, you know. Asking them about the day," I said before I started the car.

"You and Mr. Roberts were right. It doesn't matter if I stay here or not. What matters is knowing what I might be giving up," she said quietly. "I want the people who took care of my grandfather to know I appreciate it."

Her generous heart astounded me. She'd never met the man. He had damaged her family immeasurably. Yet she understood what he meant to the people who worked for him.

We drove in comfortable silence through the late evening sunshine to Rowan's hotel. I stopped in front of the door and turned to her. "I'll pick you up at ten-thirty tomorrow."

She sighed and smiled at me. "Thanks for taking such good care of me today, Adam."

"You're welcome. You're a breath of fresh air, Rowan Mayfield," I told her honestly.

"I never thought I'd meet a Bostonian so far from home."

"Tomorrow you can tell me what I've missed."

"I'll do that." She yawned again.

I laughed at her. "Go to bed. You'll be asleep on your feet next."

Rowan walked into the hotel, carrying her shoes in her hands. I winced at the blisters on the back of her heels. Tomorrow would be a better day for her. I'd make sure of it.

Chapter 7

Rowan

I really did intend to eat breakfast, but I slept through it. I also slept through the alarm and the second alarm. I only woke when someone banged hard on the door.

I raised my head, blinking sleepily, not sure what had disturbed me.

"Ms. Mayfield! Ms. Mayfield! Are you awake?" I vaguely recognized the voice belonging to the young receptionist.

"Uh...yeah." I was now.

"It's ten-thirty. Your friend, Adam, is waiting downstairs for you."

I sat bolt upright. Oh no! "Tell him I'll be down in ten minutes."

"Okay."

I heard footsteps walk away as I ran into the bathroom and stepped into the shower. After I was blasted with cold water, I was certainly awake and cursing. My mom would have scolded me for the language. Once the water warmed, I had the quickest shower I could manage, then dressed in jeans and a light pink summer shirt.

I winced as my sneakers rubbed the back of my heels through my socks. I needed to find a pharmacy before I did any walking. I quickly brushed and tied my hair back, then looked out the window and decided to grab my hoody. I had been warned about English summers.

I checked the clock before I left the room. A little over ten minutes. That would do.

I found Adam talking animatedly to the receptionist at the front desk as I approached. Then he spotted me and smiled. "I guess I didn't have to worry about you getting a good night's sleep."

I gave him a sheepish smile. "I guess not. I missed breakfast."

Adam held up a brown paper bag. "Breakfast from the hotel. Pastries. And I have a present."

I blinked. "You do?"

He juggled the bag, then held out his palm and unfolded his fingers, to show two bandages. "I thought you might need these. They're for your blisters."

"You angel." I limped over to a chair, sat down, and kicked off my sneakers and pulled back my socks. The bandages just about covered the blisters.

"I've got more if you need them," he said, joining me in the chair opposite.

"You must be fed up with taking care of me." I slipped on the sneakers and sighed with relief. That was better.

"I've also got coffee in the car. Mom made it."

"You can't be real," I muttered. "Coffee, breakfast, and bandages?" Then I realized how ungracious that sounded. "I mean—"

Adam rolled his eyes. "You're just hangry.

Come on, you can eat while I drive and tell you what we're gonna do."

I shut up. Seriously. It was better than getting myself into more trouble.

In the car, Adam refused to drive until I'd drunk a cup of coffee and eaten a pastry.

"You'll throw it over yourself if I drive now," he pointed out.

I scowled at him, but it was only half-hearted. With my luck he was probably right. I had to admit I felt more human once I had food and coffee inside me.

"Mom won't let me drive unless I've eaten breakfast," Adam confessed. "She says it's not fair to other road users."

I laughed. "My mom used to insist I ate breakfast too, but that was so I didn't shout at my bosses and lose my job."

"I sense a pattern here," Adam said.

"We both have anger issues?"

"Nope," he said cheerfully. "Bossy moms."

I giggled because he was so right.

"Not that I'd ever tell her that."

"I won't give you away," I assured him.

"I knew there was a reason I liked you. Are you ready to face Charlie?"

"Is anyone ever ready to face Charlie?"

I'd meant it as a joke, but Adam gave me a serious look. "If you get Charlie on your side, the rest of the estate will follow."

I held back the cracks about Charlie being the Pied Piper, because I knew Adam was trying to tell me something important. Don't screw this up.

Charlie mattered. I felt butterflies in my stomach. It was like I was going to an interview for the job of my dreams. I guessed it *was* an interview in a way. They were making sure I was fit to take over the Mayfield family and estate. At least this time I had a friend beside me.

As if Adam knew what I was thinking, he patted my knee. "Be yourself, Rowan Mayfield. You'll do fine."

I really hoped so. I realized even after one day Adam's opinion mattered to me. He'd rescued me from a bad situation and now I didn't want to let him down.

We drove onto the estate using yet another gate. He headed to a part of it I didn't recognize and pulled up in front of a new one-story building, near what looked like an old barn.

Adam caught me studying the buildings. "The estate office is new. The old building was ready to fall down. William turned a deaf ear to Charlie asking for repairs, then a tree fell down in high winds and the whole building collapsed."

I gasped. "Was anyone hurt?"

That had to have been frightening.

"No, but Charlie was furious. William realized he couldn't afford to keep ignoring the upkeep of the estate."

I looked at Adam. Was he trying to tell me something here? "Was it lack of money?"

He caught my gaze. "No, lack of will. William was old and tired. I think he thought the next generation could pick up the pieces. But repairs couldn't wait."

"And the rest of the estate?"

He huffed. "It needs work. There's nothing majorly wrong, but it's old and tired like William."

I nodded, trying to hide my fear. I was an outsider from a small apartment in Boston. What did I know about the maintenance of a huge country estate in England? I had the sudden urge to ask him to drive me to the airport.

Adam patted my knee. "Listen to Charlie. He loves talking."

"You'll stay by my side?"

"Sure will." Adam smirked at me. "I know it's gonna annoy Charlie."

"Of all the fake fiancés I had to choose you."

"Ya got me!"

We grinned at each other and the tension inside me eased. I had a question I needed answering though.

"Why did you agree to be my fake fiancé?"

The smile slid off Adam's face. "I don't like bullies. And they were gonna bully you out of what is rightfully yours. What William wanted. I know them and individually they're good people." He must have seen my dubious expression. "They are. Even Willow. But the minute you mention family, they become this united pack. I've seen it before, and I wasn't going to let them do it again."

I was about to question him further when there was a knock at my window. I jumped so hard I nearly shed my skin. I turned to see a middle-aged man wearing a tweed cap grinning at me.

"Charlie, I presume."

Adam snorted. "You presume right. Come on.

He probably gave up waiting for us to get out of the car."

I opened the car door. "Hi, Charlie. I've heard a lot about you. I'm Rowan."

Charlie's eyes crinkled at the edges as he smiled at me. "Hi Rowan. I've heard a lot about you too, but nothing from your fiancé here."

"Like I would tell you about my private life," Adam scoffed, but I could see the laughter in his eyes.

I waggled my eyebrows at the estate manager. "Can you tell me about Adam?"

Charlie's eyes lit up. "What do you want to know?"

"Everything," I said to the sound of Adam's groan.

"You've come to the right place," Charlie assured me. He guided me into the office, leaving Adam grumbling behind us.

I looked over my shoulder and smirked at Adam. He dropped me a wink. I took a deep breath and smiled. I could do this.

By the time we had coffee in front of us, Charlie had apparently exhausted his knowledge of Adam and he had other things he wanted to discuss. Like me and my inheritance. I saw Adam lean against the wall. I guess he wanted to stay out of the conversation. It was up to me to handle Charlie.

Charlie fixed me with a piercing gaze. "Why are you here, Ms. Mayfield?"

"Rowan," I said firmly.

"Rowan."

"I'm here because Adam suggested I needed to know what I was giving up if I went home." I hadn't intended to be so honest, but I had the feeling the man would see through any prevarication. From the way both men nodded their heads I had made the right decision.

"What do you know about the estate?"

"Nothing," I admitted. "My mom and Gran refused to talk about the family, and it was nothing to me." I sipped at my coffee and tried not to let the familiar anger boil up inside me whenever I thought about how my Gran and Mom had suffered.

Charlie hummed. "You've met some of the staff already."

"I met Alfie and Barry last night at the pub."

Was this a test?

"You impressed them."

I looked him square in the eye. "I'm not trying to impress people, Charlie. I want to get to know them. I'm not like the family. I'm just a receptionist from Boston."

"You're not like them," Charlie agreed. "But there's some of William in you. I heard you faced down Willow."

I shrugged, not really sure what to say to that. These people had known each other for years. I didn't mind talking about what the family had done to me, but I wasn't going to be rude about his employer to his face.

Charlie gave a nod. "Rowan, let me show you what being a Mayfield is all about."

I smiled at him. "I'd love that. Thanks, Charlie."

Adam heaved off the wall, ready to join us, but Charlie shook his head. "Not you, matey. You've got work to do. I'll take care of your girl for the day."

"But—" Adam started.

"The south flowerbed needs weeding," Charlie said. "Off you go."

Adam came over to me, knelt beside me, and took my hands. "Are you all right about this? I won't leave you if you don't want me too."

I wasn't sure how I felt about being separated from Adam, but I couldn't expect him to stay by my side forever or not do his job. If I went home, he'd be in a difficult position. "I'll see you later."

He looked at me, I think testing my resolve, then he nodded. "Charlie can drop you by the south flowerbed when you're finished.

I furrowed my brow. "I thought the estate was huge."

Now Adam looked confused. "It is."

"Won't you be finished before us?"

He chuckled. "The south flowerbed is huge. I'll still be there. That's why he's sent me there."

I looked at Charlie who smirked at me. "You're sending him there to get rid of him?"

"You catch on quickly."

Adam disappeared with a wave, leaving me with the estate manager.

I took a deep breath and focused my attention on Charlie. "Where do we go first?"

"Come with me," Charlie said cheerfully.

I left the office and followed him to the Land Rover with the Mayfield crest of arms on the side.

Once we got into the vehicle, Charlie turned to me, his expression serious.

"Why are you here?"

I wrinkled my brow. "I thought I'd answered that question."

Charlie shook his head. "Why did you come to the funeral?"

"I told you. I was summoned," I said, an edge to my voice.

"You could have ignored the invitation."

"I wanted to know who'd wrecked my Gran's and Mom's lives."

Charlie nodded. "Fair enough. That's honest, at least. Don't you do the same to Adam. He's a good kid."

I wanted to laugh because no way could Adam be described as a kid, but Charlie was deadly serious.

"I won't hurt Adam," I promised.

"You'd better not. He loves his family and he's a hard worker. If you screw up with this fake fiancé nonsense, it's Adam and his family that will pay the price."

"I understand," I said.

Charlie pressed his lips together. "I'm not sure that you do, but you will."

We took off down the drive before I had a chance to respond.

Chapter 8

Adam

After the excitement of the day before, it was soothing weeding the flower bed. It was warm enough for me to strip off my jacket and roll up my shirtsleeves. I wiped the sweat off my forehead with the back of my hand and wished I'd brought a bottle of water with me. Maybe there was one in the Honda. I usually kept drinks and snacks in the trunk.

I grew the tall flowers for the vases in the main house in this flowerbed. The weeding was comfortably mindless, and my thoughts kept drifting to Rowan. I hope she managed to hold her own against Charlie who was a force of nature. I wasn't a fool. I knew why Charlie wanted to question Rowan without me being there to defend her.

I'd only known Rowan for two days, but I felt fiercely protective of her. I'd never felt like this about any woman before. From the moment I saw her peering over the railing of the balcony I knew I wanted to get to know her. I smiled as I eased a dandelion out of the bed. Charlie was going to find out he wasn't the only force of nature. I was sure Rowan could hold her own. I hoped she could, because if he hurt her, I was going to hunt him down.

Then I dug fiercely at the bindweed we could never get on top of. Maybe threatening my boss wouldn't be a good idea.

"But if he hassles her, he'll hear it from me," I muttered.

"He didn't hassle me—much," Rowan said, obviously amused.

And of course she would overhear me.

I turned to face her and looked her up and down. "You seem to be in one piece."

Rowan chuckled. "He just wanted to know my intentions."

I raised an eyebrow. "Your intentions?"

"I assured him they were strictly honorable. Water?" She handed me an ice-cold bottle. "Charlie said you forgot this."

I sighed in pleasure as I uncapped the bottle. "He was right." The cool water was very welcome as it slid down my throat.

Rowan blushed as I caught her watching me drink.

"I'm always right," Charlie boomed as he joined us, distracting both of us.

"I wouldn't go that far," I muttered.

Charlie shoved me hard, and I'd have landed in my freshly weeded flowerbed if it hadn't been for Rowan grabbing me.

I thanked her and then scowled at Charlie. "What was that for? My boss will kill me if I squash the gladioli."

Rowan grinned. "Which ones are the glad—glad—whatever you said."

"Gladioli," I supplied. "The cerise pink ones."

"My mom would have known. She used to look at pictures of gardens and tell me she would have a small yard of her own one day." Rowan looked around her. "She would have loved to be in a garden like this." I heard the wistfulness in Rowan's voice.

I looked at the formal gardens stretching all the way to the lawn, gardens I'd spent hours weeding and pruning to look wonderful.

"I wish I could have shown your mom around the gardens," I said gently.

"Me too," she said, sniffling a little, her eyes suspiciously bright, holding back the tears.

Charlie coughed and patted Rowan's back. "It's thanks to Adam and his team they look so good. He works like a trojan."

I smiled at him. "Thanks, Charlie."

"He's a total pain of course," he continued, "but he works hard."

"You couldn't have stopped with the nice words?" I complained.

"Why would I do that?" he scoffed. Then he smirked at Rowan. "It's been good to meet you, Rowan. You're just what this place needs."

Rowan's eyes widened. "You mean that?"

"I do. It's time this place was shaken up a bit. You've got good ideas."

I grinned from ear to ear. I knew introducing Rowan to Charlie was a good idea.

"And you don't need to look so smug," he said to me.

"I have good ideas too," I pointed out.

Charlie growled and stomped off in the direction of the office, but he couldn't hide his smile.

I laughed at his retreating back, and Rowan joined in. It was good to see her happy and relaxed.

"Hey, would you like a late lunch?" I asked. "Mom made us sandwiches."

"Your mom made me lunch too?"

"She did. This is a one-off," I added hastily. "I usually go home for lunch, but I didn't know how long you'd be with Charlie."

"I'm starving," she confessed. "I think Charlie brought me back because my stomach kept growling."

"Come this way."

I led her back to the Honda and pulled out an insulated green bag decorated with pears and another flask.

"More coffee?" Rowan asked.

I gave a wry smile. "I run on coffee. This garden was created with caffeine, and this is my favorite spot."

I led her around the corner to a little nook in the rose garden with a stone bench and a view across the valley.

"I always hide in here when I don't want to be found," I confessed.

Rowan flopped down onto the bench with a relieved sigh. "You might end up sharing the space."

"I can live with that," I assured her, and she gave me a sweet smile.

I offered her the coffee and unzipped the bag. "I don't think you'll be hungry. Mom has packed enough for four."

Her eyes lit up. "Bring it on!"

I laid out the sandwiches, the chicken, potato salad, and chips between us on the bench.

Rowan gave a happy sigh. "I love your mom."

I loved my mom too, even if she did nose into my private life a little more than I'd like.

"So how did you get on with Charlie?" I asked around a bite of sandwich.

"I need more than a couple of hours with him," Rowan admitted. "He knows so much. He told me about the history of the Mayfields, and how the estate had developed. It's fascinating."

Her eyes sparkled and the sun picked out the red strands in her hair. I was quickly falling for Rowan Mayfield.

"You like the history, huh?" I asked before she caught me staring like a teenager. "Chips?"

At Rowan's nod, I split a bag and put it between us. "You're lucky. Mom didn't give us any of the weird Brit flavors like prawn cocktail or Marmite." I laughed as she shuddered.

"It's good to know what I'm up against," she admitted.

"You mean the family?"

"And the chips. But yeah, the family. It makes it more personal." She gave a rueful smile. "I can see why they're annoyed about it being handed to an outsider. It's generations of history being handed to a stranger."

I hummed. "Remember you're as much family

as they are. William was your grandfather."

"But it should have gone to Uncle Raymond as the next male heir. Isn't that what happens? Admittedly my knowledge is confined to historical romance novels that Gran used to read. But I know women don't usually inherit."

"Maybe William thought he'd given the estate to the best person," I suggested.

Rowan furrowed her brow. "He knew nothing about me. I never spoke to him and nor did my mom."

I didn't want to argue with her, but I'd gotten to know William in the time I'd been here. "Maybe he knew more than you think. William was old, not stupid. He wouldn't have given the estate to just anyone. He thought you were worth it, Rowan."

She nodded her head slowly. "That's what Charlie said, with more curse words."

I snorted because that was so Charlie. "He knew William too. They fished together."

"William liked fishing?"

"William and Harry like fishing. Willow does too, but she knew the men liked guy time."

Rowan chewed on her bottom lip. "Maybe she would take me. I like fishing too."

"You fish?" I couldn't imagine when Rowan would have had the chance to learn in the city.

"My mom had a friend. He used to take me when she was working and needed a babysitter. He didn't really know what to do with a kid, so he took me fishing."

"See, you've already got something in common

with the family."

I ate a handful of chips, relishing the salty goodness, while I watched a myriad of expressions cross her face. I could see she struggled with the idea of having anything in common with her English family.

She picked at the chips one by one. "It's hard listening to you talk about them, you know? You keep showing me their human side. It's easier to hate them for what they did to Mom and me."

That was a very honest admission and I owed her an honest response.

"If I were in your place, I'd feel the same way. As I said, individually they're good people, but the Family™ is a different matter."

"You think I should get to know the family?" Rowan asked. "I don't know what to do. If I stay away much longer, I'm going to lose my jobs. I can change the flight, I guess, but I've got nowhere to stay, and no money."

I heard a stone scatter across the path and looked up to see Willow, her attention on Rowan. I hadn't heard her approach until that moment. I wondered if she'd heard Rowan's comment.

"Rowan."

Rowan sat up straight. "Willow."

Willow's expression tightened. "The family has been talking and we've agreed a trial period for you and your...fiancé."

Would it kill the family to offer an olive branch without conditions? Then I remembered I was supposed to be Rowan's fiancé.

"A trial period? For what?" Rowan demanded.

"This isn't a job. The estate is *mine*. If anything, I should be offering *you* the trial period."

I groaned inwardly. Well, this was going well. I was tempted to call my mom and ask her to mediate. She was more likely to smack their heads together. Maybe I should try that.

"Ms. Mayfield." I tried for formal first. "Rowan needs somewhere to stay."

"I don't think—" Willow started.

"Rowan wants to get to know you and there's plenty of room in the house."

I turned to Rowan and saw her wary expression. "We can get your things from the hotel. You can change your flight so that it's open-ended."

I didn't mention the lack of money in front of Willow. Rowan could talk to the solicitor about that.

Willow pressed her lips together. "You're right, of course. I'll arrange it. You should come for dinner tonight." She added, "Both of you," reluctantly.

My fiancée looked as if she wanted to bolt. I leaned over and took her hand. "Thank you," I said, nudging Rowan.

She startled, as if she'd been lost in thought. "Uh...yes...thank you, Willow. I'll look forward to it."

Rowan really needed acting lessons.

I smiled at Willow. "We'll see you just before six." I knew the time the family ate dinner.

Willow gave a curt nod and stalked away.

Rowan turned on me. "Are you mad? You're

throwing me into the lions' den. Those wolves will tear me apart."

I squinted at her. "I'm confused. Wolves or lions?"

"Does it matter?" she snapped.

"I guess not." I took Rowan's hands. "Rowan, this makes sense. If you stay elsewhere the family can shut you out, exclude you. This way they've got to get to know you."

"What about my jobs? Money?"

I realized it was down to me to do the hard talking. "I know you don't want to hear this, but that part of your life is over. You'll be a rich woman whatever happens."

I saw the hurt and anger and fear in her eyes. My girl didn't know where to turn.

"I don't have a dime to my name," she said quietly.

I wanted to take her in my arms, but I held back, knowing she wasn't in the mood for that. "We'll sort that, I promise. You're not on your own, Rowan. You have me to help you."

Chapter 9

Rowan

I clung onto Adam's hand as we climbed the stone stairs to the huge, carved, double front doors. He held my carry-on in his other hand. I'd only brought a small case. I hadn't intended to stay more than a few days.

"Are you sure about this?" I said, glancing at Adam.

I thought how smart he looked in a pale-blue, button-down shirt and dark pants. He'd twirled around when he picked me up from the hotel.

"Look, no dirt, Mom."

I rolled my eyes and then shoved him. Well, someone had to.

I was grateful I'd packed a light floral dress which I'd bought on impulse but had never worn. It was smart enough to look formal. I had to wear my sneakers though. There was no way I could wear the shoes with my blisters.

Adam gave my hand a comforting squeeze. "Hiding away from the family isn't going to help you or them get to know each other."

"Well, then, fake fiancé, you'd better be by my side the whole time."

"I won't let go of you, I promise. If it's any consolation, they're probably as scared of you as you are of them."

I scoffed. "Why would they be scared of me?"

"You could bring their cushy lifestyle tumbling around their ears," he pointed out.

"Not if they contest the will."

"They have more to lose than you."

I thought about that as we went into the house. Adam was right in a way. I had nothing to start with. They had everything. If this truly was a rags-to-riches story, would it kill me to be nice to them? In the movies there was always a happy ever after.

Except this wasn't the movies and I was petrified.

I hadn't paid much attention to the house when I'd arrived for the funeral. But now I looked up at the sweeping carved oak staircase and carved panels on the walls Charlie had told me came from oak trees on the estate. Oak seemed to feature heavily in the décor. It wasn't my taste, but it was elegant. My Mom would have loved it. A wave of anger swept over me, and Adam turned to look at me.

"Are you okay?"

"Yeah," I muttered, and he narrowed his eyes. I sighed. "I'm fine. It's just hard, you know. Every time I think of my mom it makes me angry."

Adam tugged me against his side and wrapped his arm around my shoulders. It was very comforting, and I leaned in. We stood in the massive hallway. No one had come to greet us, not even a member of staff. So much for welcoming the new member of the family.

"Where is everybody?" I asked.

"I'm here."

I turned to see a tall, balding man dressed much like Adam hurrying across the hall. This was Harry. I didn't know much about him, except that Adam seemed to like him.

"I'm so sorry, my dear. Willow asked me to greet you, as it's Robin's day off, but I got involved in a mission and lost track of time."

I blinked. Who was Robin? A mission? I turned to Adam for help.

"Mr. Mayfield plays video games," he told me. "Robin is the butler."

Harry made a *pfft* sound and waved his hand. "No need to be formal, Adam. We're all family here."

That remained to be seen, but I was glad he hadn't called Adam by his last name.

"Harry is really good at video games," Adam assured me.

Harry must have caught my speculative glance. "Do you play?"

"I do, although I've not had much chance recently," I admitted.

Harry's eyes lit up and he held out his arm. "Come to my study, Rowan. Adam, leave Rowan's suitcase by the stairs. We can take it up later."

Adam did as Harry suggested.

Harry grinned at me. "We've got a short while before dinner. We can talk games and bore Adam to death."

I glanced at Adam. "You don't play?"

"I'd rather watch paint dry," he muttered.

I grinned at him. "Poor Adam. Lead the way, Harry."

I tucked my hand into the crook of his elbow and let him lead me across the hall the way he'd come, but I was pleased Adam stayed by my side as he'd promised.

Harry didn't just *like* games. They'd obviously been a lifelong addiction. Where some people had shelves of books, Harry had shelves of video games, spanning forty or more years. Adam sat in one of the wingback chairs by the fire, while Harry took me around the room. It was like being in a museum. He had the games and the video consoles to play them.

"Oh Harry," I breathed. "This is..." I didn't even have the words to say what this was.

He beamed at my open admiration. I'd obviously made him happy.

"What are you playing now?" I asked.

He pointed to the huge screen on the wall, frozen in mid-explosion. My eyes lit up. This was a game I recognized.

"We could play now?" he asked hopefully.

"Willow's going to be furious," Adam pointed out. "You know how cross she gets when you miss dinner."

Harry's shoulders slumped and he sighed. It was adorable to see this fifty-something man pouting as if he were a teenage girl.

But he nodded. "Adam's right. She's always having a go at me for missing a meal. Willow insists we eat together."

"Another time," I suggested, and was rewarded

with a huge smile.

"Harry, where are you? Is Rowan here yet?" Willow called out.

"In my study." Harry grimaced. "Don't tell her I forgot about greeting you."

"It'll be our secret," I promised, patting his arm.

Adam and Charlie liked Harry and I was beginning to understand why. There was a kind of innocence about him I liked. I could see why maybe he wasn't the right person to manage the Mayfield Estate. But I also remembered what Adam had said. Individually the family were fine, but together was a different matter. I needed to see the bigger picture.

Willow walked in, her heels clicking on the floorboards. "Rowan. I hope Harry's not been boring you."

I smiled at Harry and then at Willow. "Not at all. I love playing video games."

She sighed at the same time as Adam. I managed not to burst out laughing but it was a close-run thing.

"Dinner is ready," Willow announced.

I followed Willow out of the study. Once in the hall, Adam and Harry flanked me, which was comforting. I had my protectors. I sought Adam's hand again and he laced his fingers in mine.

I expected a formal dinner with more cutlery than I'd ever seen. What I got was dinner around the kitchen table with Ash doing the cooking. The kitchen was huge, at least the size of my apartment and surprisingly modern with stainless steel appliances. But the table was old and well-used. I imagined my aunts and uncles sitting around here as children. I wondered if any of them had kids of their own. None of them appeared to be married.

Ash looked over her shoulder as we came in. "Hi Rowan," she said cheerfully, blowing a strand of gray hair out of her mouth. Her face was flushed, and her long hair escaped the confines of its bun. She was dressed in a blouse and jeans and looked nothing like the tall, elegant woman I'd met at the funeral. "Sorry, you've got me cooking this evening. Jo is out with Robin."

"Jo is the cook," Adam told me before I had to ask. "She's married to Robin."

"Ash is the best cook out of all of us," Harry confided, "so we voted her to make the meal. Willow would have poisoned you."

"Yes, well, Rowan doesn't need to hear that." But Willow's lips twitched, and I could see my aunt was trying to hide a smile.

The knot of tension that had been in my chest all day eased and I felt as if I could breathe for the first time. They were making an effort to welcome me in their own way.

I looked at the table. Five places. "Is Raymond joining us?"

"He sends his apologies, but he's got a prior engagement," Willow said.

Ash snorted. "He's the one who called you a tart and he's too embarrassed to show his face."

"Ash," Willow scolded.

I saw Adam's expression darken. "It's okay," I said, as much to reassure him as the family. "It was said in the heat of the moment. I'd like to meet him." He gave me a curt nod as if to tell me he'd gotten the message.

Harry patted my arm. "I'll go and call him." He vanished out of the kitchen.

"Don't take long. Dinner is ready," Ash called. "If I don't say that he'll vanish into his study and that's the last we'll see of him."

"It's very understanding of you," Willow said, her gaze piecing through me.

I shrugged. I wasn't about to admit I didn't know what a tart, other than an open pie, was. I'm sure he wasn't calling me a pastry dish. "We got off on the wrong foot."

For some reason that made Willow glance down at my feet.

"I've got blisters on both heels," I confessed.

She looked concerned. "I've got plasters if you need them."

I understood what plasters were thanks to Adam. "Thanks. Adam brought me a pack this morning."

Willow looked at Adam. It hadn't escaped my notice that she'd more or less ignored him. "Thank you for taking care of Rowan."

"It's my job," he said, taking my hand again. "As her fiancé."

She hummed. If she'd hired a plane and written it in the sky, it couldn't be more obvious she wanted to call us out on the lie.

But she didn't and then Harry returned.

"He'll be back in an hour. He's having dinner with one of the tenants."

From the lack of expression on Willow's and Ash's faces they knew who he was with. Even Adam didn't seem surprised. So I wasn't the only member of the family involved with someone on the estate. I would pump Adam for more information later.

Then Willow ushered me to the table. Adam sat next to me before Willow could make an alternative arrangement. Harry sat down opposite me and gave me a reassuring smile. I returned it. It was kind of him to put me at ease.

Then Ash put a plate down in front of me and I focused on the food. I confess, I'd been worrying about what they'd expect me to eat. Maybe they'd try to haze me. My co-workers back home had regaled me with stories British food, of Yorkshire pudding and spotted dick. So I breathed a sigh of relief when I saw slices of ham and mashed potato, peas, beans, and carrots. At least I knew what they were.

"Worried about what you were going to get?" Adam murmured.

I gave him a sheepish smile. "I like to know what I'm eating."

"Me too," Harry agreed.

"You're just fussy," Ash said to him as she put the plate in front of him.

"My gran used to say that about me until I realized she never cooked anything she didn't like to eat," I told Harry.

He gave me a grin. "The trouble with being the youngest is that your siblings have always got stories about you as a child to tell people."

I couldn't help the sad smile. I had no one left to tell tales about me. Once my mom died, I was alone in the world.

Harry's smile faded. "I'm sorry, dear, that was thoughtless of me."

To my surprise, Willow said "Maybe now you'll have other family to tell stories about you."

"Like vaulting over the balcony railing," Ash said.

"With no shoes," Harry added.

"To land in the gardener's arms," Adam finished.

I scowled at Adam. "Did you have to join in?"

"If he's going to be family of course he had to join in," Willow said brusquely. "Eat up, Rowan, before it gets cold."

I stared at the plate of food. I'd forgotten it was there.

Eat. I could do that.

Family. I wasn't sure I could do that.

Fake fiancé. My life had gotten a whole lot more complicated.

Chapter 10

Adam

I quietly seethed through dinner. I was going to make it clear to Raymond when he showed his face that he didn't get to call my girl names. The revelation had bothered me more than I expected. Rowan had been the innocent party in all of this. If they were going to be angry at anyone it should have been William and his machinations.

"Adam?" Rowan's quiet voice disturbed me from my angry thoughts.

Dinner was finished. Ash and Willow were clearing away the dirty plates. They'd declined our offer of help. Harry had disappeared. I wasn't sure where he was although I could take a guess.

"Hey, sorry, I was lost in thought," I admitted.

Rowan shot me a knowing look. "Not good ones, judging by your expression."

"Nothing important. Just thinking about the garden."

"You're still thinking about Raymond," she chided softly, obviously not wanting her aunts to overhear.

"Is it that obvious?" I said ruefully.

"You need to practice your poker face."

I sat back in the chair. "I don't like name-calling. I never have." I kept my voice low too.

"It's not important. I've been called worse. And I get that he was shocked and angry."

"You have a kind heart, Rowan."

She blushed a little. "You're the one with the kind heart. You took care of me when I needed it. Just forget it."

I shook my head. "I'll forgive, but I won't forget it. I thought more of Raymond than that."

Rowan locked gazes with me and I looked into the chocolate-velvet of her eyes.

"Break it up, you two," Willow said briskly as she put a tray with a coffee pot and five cups on the table. "You can go all lovey-dovey another time. Coffee first, then we'll get you settled in your bedroom."

I felt a shiver run through Rowan.

"It's kind of you to offer me a room," she said.

"Nonsense. You're a Mayfield. You should stay with us." Ash exchanged a glance with Willow and then looked at her niece. "We're sorry for the way we behaved at first. We were all shocked, but it's no excuse. You're as much a Mayfield as we are."

Rowan shook her head. "William never married my grandmother."

"There's no title at stake, dear," Willow said. "The Mayfields were never interested in nobility, only money. They married for industrial connections."

"What are you saying?" I asked.

Willow scowled at me, obviously not appreciating my interruption. But I wanted it laid out for everyone to see. I didn't want the family cozying up to Rowan only to stab her in the back later.

She huffed. "I'm saying we are family and should get to know each other. Nothing more, nothing less."

"Do any of you have children?" Rowan asked suddenly. "I'm sorry if that's rude, but none of you seem to be married."

"No husbands, wives, or kids," Ash said cheerfully.

"So that makes me the only one of the next generation." Rowan narrowed her eyes. "So that's why you wanted to arrange a 'suitable' match."

Willow had the grace to look embarrassed, especially when Ash turned on her.

"Seriously, Wils? You threatened her with marriage to one of those idiots?"

"The Mayfields marry for connections," Willow huffed.

"But not the sharks," Ash protested.

"You didn't," Rowan pointed out. "None of you married for connections. Why should I have to?"

"She's got you there," Ash said.

"Why didn't you all marry?" I asked, curious now.

Willow shrugged. "I never found anyone I loved enough to share the rest of my life with. Well, who wanted to share their life with me." There was a sadness there. Maybe a lost love?

"I prefer horses to people," Ash admitted.

"And Harry and Raymond?" Rowan asked.

Willow's smile was wry. "Harry never put down the video console and Raymond found someone late in life. Too late to have an heir. Father was never bothered by not having future generations."

Ash smiled ruefully. "Maybe it was because he knew he had you waiting in the wings."

I saw Rowan's expression darken. Considering what she'd been through that was less than tactful.

"Well done, Ash," Willow muttered. She handed a cup of coffee to Rowan. "Just ignore my sister. She spends all day talking to horses. She's clearly forgotten how to talk to humans.

Ash furrowed her brow, clearly confused, then her eyes went wide. "I'm so sorry, Rowan. I didn't mean to imply...oh goodness, I've really made a mess of this."

Rowan shook her head. "No, maybe you're right. I mean William knew where I was all this time. Maybe he just was waiting for the right time, only it never happened. He must have been disappointed I wasn't a boy."

"For a traditional man," Ash said. "our father never had an issue about who the estate went to. Girl or boy. He just wanted it to go to the right person. And he thought that was you."

"Why aren't you angry still?" Rowan asked. "I would be if my father had handed my world to a stranger. We share a name, nothing else."

Willow and Ash exchanged another look.

"I am," Willow admitted. "I don't know what on earth my father was thinking handing over our life to a stranger. I want—wanted—to contest the will." She sighed and sat back in her seat. "But the hard truth is we could drag this through the courts and still lose to you. Or worse, lose the estate for all of us, the family and the staff and tenants. Is it worth the risk?"

Ash nodded. "We've done some hard talking. All four of us. We realized we need to work together, all of us, and that includes you, to make this work."

Rowan sipped her coffee cautiously, then put down her cup. "I don't know what I want to do yet. You had a point. I don't belong here."

I decided to intervene before Rowan inadvertently handed them an ace to play. I would only trust them so far. "You don't belong here *yet*, sweetheart. But there is time and I'll be by your side."

I pressed my leg against Rowan's in the hope she'd get the message I was trying to send her. There was a hesitation, then she pressed against my leg. Message received.

"How's your dad, Adam?" Ash asked.

I knew my face tightened by the way Rowan leaned into me to be the one to give me comfort. "He's a fighter."

"If he needs anything, just ask us."

"I will. Getting the hospital bed has made a huge difference. Thank you."

Ash's lips twitched. "What a surprise that our acting gardener is affianced to our new niece."

"Isn't it," Rowan murmured.

"But we know you've taken care of Rowan and introduced her to Charlie. We should have done that."

"You haven't had time to think about playing auntie to a new niece," I said, wanting to play nice. "You've just buried your only parent and you've got this huge estate to manage."

Rowan sighed. "Willow, Ash, could we start over?"

"On one condition," Willow said.

I tensed, not sure what she was going to say.

"What's that?" Rowan asked, sounding as wary as me.

"You call us Aunt Willow and Aunt Ash. Show your aunts some respect." But she was smiling.

Rowan bit her lip. "How about when I'm comfortable with you being my family, I'll call you aunt."

"We can accept that." Ash said.

Willow looked as if she wanted to argue but she nodded reluctantly. "I can work with that."

"Where did Harry go?" Rowan asked.

Ash groaned. "Two guesses and there's no sign of Raymond."

"We won't see Raymond. He's got no idea of timing," Willow said with a resignation borne of long experience. "If Harry has stepped into his study, that's the last we'll see of him all evening. I'll show you your room. I saw your case by the stairs. I'm guessing Harry didn't get around to that."

"We got...uh...distracted," Rowan said.

"It turns out your niece is a huge video game player, just like Harry," I said.

Willow knocked her forehead on the table. "Not another one."

"She loves fishing," I said.

"There, there, Wils," Ash cooed, patting her sister's back. "Fishing and video games. Rowan fits right in."

"I'm with you, Willow. I hate them too," I said.

"At least someone has some sense," Willow muttered into the table.

Rowan looked at me as if I were nuts. "I can't believe you don't play games."

I smirked at her. "I do play games. Just not the ones you're thinking of."

"Adam's a mischievous one," Ash said, "but you probably know that already."

"I do now," Rowan agreed, and she smirked right back.

We finished the pot of coffee and despite the hard conversation which wasn't really resolved, Rowan looked more relaxed, and the strain in her face had eased.

Then she yawned and grimaced. "I think I'm still jetlagged."

"You should have an early night," Willow said.

After a pointed silence, and a hard stare from Willow, I realized that was my cue to leave. I was reluctant to leave Rowan at their mercies. From the look on Rowan's face, she felt the same way.

Ash looked between the two of us and snorted. "Your *fiancée* will be fine, Adam. We won't eat her."

"I'll walk you out to the car," Rowan said.

She laced her fingers in mine as we walked across the hall. "Will I see you tomorrow?"

"I'll be in the formal gardens all morning. If you need me, you can find me there. But I'd like to take you to Mom's for lunch."

Her smile was bright in the gloom of the

hallway. "I'd like that."

I stopped and turned to face her. "If you need me at all, anytime, you can call me." We'd exchanged numbers earlier in the day.

"I will," she agreed.

I leaned forward and brushed a kiss on her lips. "Sleep well."

Rowan yawned in my face. "I'm so sorry."

I turned her around and gently pushed her toward the stairs where Willow and Ash just 'happened' to be waiting. "See you tomorrow, Rowan."

I saw the big doors close in the rearview mirror as I drove away. Rowan would be all right, I knew that. But I'd thrown her into the lion's den. Would she survive?

I opened the front door of the cottage and popped my head into Dad's room. He was asleep as usual. Dad had spent most of his time sleeping during this round of chemo.

I found Mom sitting at the table in the kitchen, the newspaper in front of her. She liked doing the crossword after dinner. It was something her Mom had enjoyed doing. But she wasn't focused on the paper, and I heard her sniffle.

"Mom? What's wrong?" I rushed over and knelt beside her.

She wiped her eyes, forcing a smile. "Hi, sweetheart. How did the meal go?"

"It was good. Better than I expected," I admitted. "Why are you crying?"

Mom flapped her hand. "Just ignore me. I'm just having a weak moment."

"You're the strongest woman I know," I said. "Did the doctor come today?"

"This morning. She said Dad was doing well."

I pressed my lips together. The doctor always said that. "Has he been awake today?"

"Some," Mom said, although she refused to look at me. "This afternoon. We watched TV together."

Which meant Mom had watched her shows while Dad had slept.

"I want to introduce Rowan to Dad," I said.

"Of course, bring her around for lunch tomorrow."

I stood, groaning a little at the stiffness in my lower back from the weeding earlier. Back in Boston I went to the gym most days, but I didn't get a chance here. "I'm going to sit with Dad." I hadn't gotten a chance yesterday to be with him.

Mom looked up at me, her eyes suspiciously bright. "Thanks, son. I know he likes it when you talk about the garden. Although maybe you've got something else to talk about today?"

From on the verge of tears to wicked grin, my mother would never change. I rolled my eyes and went to tell my father all about the…garden, Mom's giggle following me.

Chapter 11

Rowan

I walked up the sweep of the main staircase, with Willow and Ash flanking me. Were they ready to haul me back if I turned and bolted? Maybe they had a point. I was so nervous I'd have begged Adam to take me with him if I'd had anywhere to sleep.

I should have kept the sweet, little hotel room for another night. This huge house wasn't me, with the cooks and gardeners and the grounds that stretched out further than the eye could see. Maybe there was an elephant graveyard in the shadows. I snorted at my ridiculous thoughts. This wasn't a *Disney* movie, and my uncles weren't going to set hyenas on me. But this wasn't me. I'd have been content to stay in a little cottage with roses around the door.

Willow stopped me and pointed at the huge portrait ahead of us. "This is your grandfather."

I gazed up at the elderly man with hair as white as snow. From the erect pose and head held high, it must have been painted before he'd gotten sick. William had been distinguished with strong features, an aquiline nose and strong jaw. I could see my mother in his eyes and the curve of his mouth. I had the same dark-brown eyes framed by long lashes, as did Willow and Ash. But there the family resemblance stopped. According to my mom, I looked more like my no-good father who'd vanished before I was born. Like mother, like daughter, my mom always said.

"It was painted five years ago," Willow said, drawing me back to the present.

"It's good," I mumbled, not sure what to say. "I don't know much about art, but I can see the life in him."

"Our father was always full of life. That's what made the last couple of years so hard for him and us." Willow grimaced as if reliving unpleasant memories. "His body crumbled but his mind was sharp."

I couldn't imagine what that was like. Watching the world carry on while your body failed. I felt an unexpected sympathy for William.

"Your uncle Harry painted the portrait," Ash said, distracting me from my thoughts.

I turned to her in surprise. "Harry is an artist?"

"He is. Mainly oils, although he dabbles in watercolors. A lot of the paintings in the house are his." Ash laughed at my shock. "You were expecting the house to be full of Rembrandts and Picassos?"

"Well, yes," I admitted, blushing. I had made that assumption.

"This is a home first," Willow said brusquely. "Harry's paintings mean more to us than an overpriced old master."

"And we're less likely to be burgled," Ash said. "The family owns a lot of art, but most pieces are loaned to galleries and museums with better security than we have here."

I realized that once again Adam was right. I'd made assumptions about my new family, and I knew nothing about them. This was a home to four people. My family. I needed to get to know them individually and together.

I suddenly remembered something I'd been meaning to ask all evening. "I've got to ask, why are the girls named after trees and the boys something traditional?"

Ash chuckled. "The original Mayfield who settled here was a keen horticulturist, responsible for planting the estate. He was the one who wanted all his children named after trees."

"So what changed?"

"His wife objected, and they compromised. The boys got family names and the girls got the trees."

"But why did it carry on?" I asked.

"Families are funny like that, dear," Willow murmured. "They like their traditions. Come on, let's get you settled."

She carried on up the stairs and I followed her, Ash by my side.

Willow walked down the hall and opened a door. "This way."

Ash ushered me into the bedroom. I gasped at the size of the room.

"I think the bed is bigger than my apartment," I murmured, clutching my carryon to me.

"This was Father's room," Ash said, taking my case and putting it down on the bed.

My eyes widened in horror. "No, I can't stay

here. It wouldn't be right. Haven't you got another room? Something smaller? For one of the staff?"

I was intimidated enough by the size of the sleigh bed, but the bedroom was huge, much larger than the kitchen. It was very masculine, decorated in browns and greens, with gold and brown drapes. A large dark brown leather couch was at an angle by the fireplace. The hearth was swept. I guess there was no need for a fire at this time of year. A stormy seascape graced the wall above the fire.

Ash put an arm around my shoulders. "We've all got suites of our own, Rowan. This is the only suite that's free. The bed is new. Harry and Willow replaced it after Dad passed away. We thought as you were American, you'd be used to big beds."

I thought of my small queen bed at home. This was at least three times the size. But it was a relief to know I wasn't sharing the bed with my grandfather and generations of Mayfields before him.

"Just go to bed and relax. There's a TV in the cabinet here if you want to watch it. The bathroom is through there, next to the dressing room." Ash pointed at a door opposite the bed, slightly ajar. "And you have a living area through there. You need to sleep. We'll see you in the morning."

Willow nodded at me and followed Ash out of the room. Not sure what to do next, I turned around, surveying the bedroom. There wasn't a lot of furniture and what was there looked practical rather than stylish. Two inlaid armoires on the long wall, a tall wooden chest with a huge mirror above it. My entire pack wouldn't fill half a drawer.

I poked my head into the bathroom, relieved to see a shower, and a tub large enough for four. The dressing room I discovered was a large closet with shelves along two sides and a long mirror. I caught my reflection in the glass. I looked like a bewildered owl, with huge, tired eyes.

Then I opened the door to the living area. It was a comfortable room, with dark green fabric couches and matching wingback chairs around the fire. Another seascape graced the wall above the mantelpiece. I was more interested in the bookcases at the end of the room. I'd explore them tomorrow. The room had a strangely impersonal feel, as if it hadn't been inhabited for a long time. Maybe William had been too ill to use the room.

The whole suite lacked a personal touch, a sense of who William had been. I guessed the rooms had been cleared for guests like me, but I was saddened by not getting to know my grandfather in his personal space.

I was exhausted but still too wired to sleep. I walked over to look out of the window. It was almost dark and the only thing I could see were a few lights in the far distance. I wondered if they were the cottages where Adam lived. I had no idea, but it was a comforting thought that Adam could be one of the lights.

I watched the lights as the darkness deepened and I yawned until my jaw cracked. I turned to face the bed. I could hold a party in there. I sighed. The party would have to wait. I just wanted to sleep.

I woke, hearing my name being called. I was disorientated, and for a moment I couldn't work out where the calling was coming from. There was no one in the room and I hadn't heard a knock at the door. Then there was a spray of something at the window which made the pane rattled. Concerned a stone was about to shatter the glass, I leapt out of bed and rushed to the window. I opened it and looked outside.

"Morning, miss!" Adam saluted me, his green eyes sparkling in the sunshine. "Nice PJ's." He looked far too wide awake for this time in the morning. He was wearing that ugly hat again which just made him look adorably cute.

I rushed back for my robe. I wore my only pair of pajamas, a floral silk camisole and shorts that my grandmother had bought me. I'd refused to wear them and stuffed them at the back of my closet. But I brought them on impulse, thinking I might need something more civilized than the shabby old T-shirt and shorts I usually wore in bed. I wrapped my robe around me, ignoring Adam's knowing smirk.

"Morning, Adam." There was no way I was calling my fake fiancé by his last name. "Did you bring me breakfast?"

He tsked. "Bring a girl breakfast once and she expects it every day.

I raised an eyebrow.

He sighed and held up a bag. "Coffee and pastries from the kitchen."

"You stole from the kitchen?" I mock-gasped.

He put a hand over his heart dramatically. "I didn't steal, ma'am. How can it be stealing when I'm feeding a member of the family? Of course if she doesn't want the coffees and pastries I can always put them back."

"Do it and die," I growled. I was really in need of caffeine.

"Then get your pretty face down here and we'll go to my hidey-hole for breakfast. Hurry up now, the coffee is getting cold."

His chuckle followed me as I raced into the bedroom to find my clothes. I squeaked a little when I realized it was nearly ten o'clock again. My body clock was really out of rhythm. I washed my face and cleaned my teeth, then raced down the stairs. It was only when I reached the hallway I realized I wasn't exactly sure which way to go to find my breakfast. I took a chance and headed through the main rooms. Sure enough, Adam was waiting under the balcony.

"How did you know I'd head this way?" I asked him.

"Lucky guess. And also the fact you have no idea which way you are going." Adam held out his arms. "Breakfast?"

This was ridiculous. But if the man wanted to catch me in his arms again, who was I to refuse? I launched myself into the air and sure enough he caught me in his strong arms, gathering me to his chest as he had once before.

He stared down at me, his eyes dark under the brim of his hat. "Hey there," he said, his voice husky.

The man took my breath away. "Hi," I gasped.

We stayed like that, me in his arms until we heard a cough and I looked round to see my aunt Ash grinning at us both.

"Morning, lovebirds," she said.

"Morning, Ash." I blushed as Adam put me on my feet.

"Good morning, Ms. Mayfield." Adam sounded far too self-assured. Obviously being caught by my aunt didn't bother him in the least.

Ash rolled her eyes. "You know I don't bother with that formal baloney, Adam. Leave that to Raymond and Willow."

"Yes, ma'am." Adam gave a slight bow.

"Cheeky boy," Ash said cheerfully. "You'd better get out of here quick. Willow is determined to show Rowan round the entire house, and Raymond has finally shown his face so expect an apology."

"He'd better," Adam growled.

I turned to look at him, but then I caught Ash's satisfied smile. "I'm sure he didn't mean—"

"Oh, he meant it, dear. But I don't think any of us covered ourselves in glory at the reading of the will. The family has some making up to do. Just let him say his apology. He'll feel a lot better for it and his blood pressure will come down." She made a shooing motion with her hands. "Now go before she catches you."

Adam held out his hand and we hurried away. I

did want a tour of the house, but not before coffee.

"I can't believe it's nearly ten o'clock again," I said. "I never sleep this late. I'm normally at work by seven in the morning."

"You'll get back into a rhythm soon enough. I'm glad you slept well."

Something in Adam's tone made me turned to look at him and I realized that under his usual bright smiles he was very tired.

"Did your dad have a bad night?" I queried, ashamed I hadn't asked him sooner.

"He was in a lot of pain," Adam said tightly. "We've called the hospice team. He wants to stay at home but we're finding it harder to manage his pain control."

He was still hanging onto my hand, and I squeezed it gently. I wanted to soothe him, but I wasn't sure how or whether he'd even welcome my comfort.

"Mom will call me later to let me know how they got on. But I really need coffee and sugar to make me feel better. How about you?"

I gave him the brightest smile I could. "Coffee and sugar sounds just about right. Where is your hidey hole?"

Adam gave me a grateful smile. "Just about...here."

We turned a corner and I stopped, rocking back on my heels. "What the—"

The small nook had been transformed, with the stone seats covered in cushions and the addition of a small table, laden with fresh juice and covered plates. But more importantly, I spied a very large pot of coffee.

I turned on Adam. "So what's in the bag?" I demanded.

Adam gave me a sheepish grin. "Dessert."

Chapter 12

Adam

The wide-eyed, shocked look on Rowan's face made it worth all the teasing from my mom as I'd begged to borrow her cushions and throws for the morning. It wasn't a candlelit dinner, I had plans for that later, but a few lush cushions and throws transformed the tiny nook. I borrowed the table from one of the sheds where it had been forgotten about. It was the perfect size.

Rowan shook her head. "I can't believe you did this for me."

I raised an eyebrow. "Who said I did it for you? I always eat my breakfast like this. Hungry?"

Her stomach growled as if I'd spoken to it directly and she blushed.

"It would be useless of me to lie now, wouldn't it?"

"Sit down!" I picked up the coffee pot. "Coffee, pastries, and strawberries and cream. Is that okay for you?"

"Pour the coffee," she growled, "before I drink it straight from the pot."

"Are you always so tetchy first thing in the morning?" I said as I poured the fragrant rich brew into the cup.

Her arched eyebrow told me I'd said something

stupid. I smacked my forehead. Of course we'd had the hangry discussion the day before. "I think I need my coffee too," I admitted ruefully.

"Pass that cup and it's all forgiven."

I did as she asked. I didn't want to make my fake fiancé unhappy with me. At least not before our first kiss.

"Juice?" I asked, pointing at the jug.

"Please."

I poured the freshly squeezed orange juice into the glasses and set one in front of Rowan. "Help yourself to anything you want."

Rowan gave a happy sigh as she selected a croissant. "This is just perfect."

I let her eat and relax for a few minutes before I asked the question that had been burning on my tongue. "How did it go last night?"

"Better than I expected," she admitted. "Willow and Ash were really kind to me. Willow is prickly, but then so was my mother. So am I," she admitted with a blush.

I mimed zipping my mouth and she poked her tongue out.

"I'm finding it hard to reconcile how nice they are to me now, with how they were when I first arrived."

I sipped at my coffee while I thought of what to say. "Prickliness does seem to be a family trait." I grinned broadly when I saw her bristle. "But they want to get to know you too. Don't knock it."

Rowan sighed. "I won't."

"You don't have to trust them, Rowan. Just give them a chance to make nice."

"I will." Rowan picked up her orange juice and gave a moan as she sipped. "This is so good."

"It should be," I agreed. "Jo makes it fresh every morning."

She squinted at me. "Are you going to get into trouble with Charlie for this? I don't want to jeopardize your job."

"It's kind of you, but I negotiated my break-time with Charlie."

I didn't tell her that my negotiations included getting up two hours earlier to make up the time. The family weren't the only ones who could drive hard bargains. Being the fake fiancé of the new leader of the estate didn't give me special privileges. Right now, this was my lunchtime.

"I think I should allow Willow to take me around the house," Rowan said, "but I've decided that I'm not gonna talk any form of financial negotiation without you and my lawyer present."

I hummed in agreement. "I think that's a good idea. Probate on an estate like this can take years so the family will need a decision from you."

"That's just it. I've got no idea what to do," she admitted.

I felt bad about pushing her. This was supposed to be a relaxing breakfast. "It's been two days. Let your solicitor handle things. You're barely over the jetlag yet. Take a deep breath, smell the roses, and drink the coffee."

As if I'd given her a command, Rowan inhaled obediently. "The roses smell amazing."

"My father and the gardeners before him picked the roses for their scent. One of the

Mayfield family was visually impaired, and the gardeners planted so that she could smell the plants even if she couldn't see them. Successive gardeners have followed that tradition."

Her face lit up as I gave her a piece of history passed on from my father.

"When Dad was well enough, he spent a lot of time telling me about the history of the gardens to make sure that I was doing my job properly. There are numerous journals and books on the subject that I can access—nothing historical is computerized—but all the gardeners have had an oral tradition of passing down the history of the planting. I just hope I'll get the same chance for whoever succeeds me after...well, just after. I can pick up a journal from any year and find out how the garden was planted that year. It's an invaluable resource."

"Why is nothing computerized?" Rowan asked.

"They've never gotten to it," I admitted. "I've been on at my dad for years to do some of the work, but he was never happy with technology."

Rowan looked speculatively at me. "Doesn't the family have an archivist?"

I blinked. "I'm sure they must have, but I don't know who it is. The house and the gardens tended to be managed very separately."

"I'll ask Willow. There must be someone who can computerize the journals. You don't want to lose all this history."

I hid my smile as I finished my coffee. Rowan was already thinking like the head of the family. I wondered if she realized it.

Conversation eased into more trivial matters then as we finished the pastries and coffee. I regaled her with more stories of my time on the estate, and she told me about her jobs in Boston. It turned out we'd lived two blocks apart and never run across each other.

"We could have had a real relationship," I said.

Rowan wrinkled her nose. "I didn't get much chance to go out when Mom was ill."

"Neither did I while I was trying to build up my business. And yet we met thousands of miles away."

"Timing," she said and our gazes locked for a long moment.

Rowan dragged her eyes away and looked at the table. "I guess we ought to clear this away. What time do you have to get back to work?"

I looked at my watch and yelped. "Fifteen minutes ago. I'm gonna have to leave you with the strawberries and cream."

Rowan shook her head. "Why don't we have that later. You go back to work, and I'll clear up here."

"We'll do it together. Keeping the garden tidy is part of my duties."

Together we cleared up the plates, small birds pecking at the crumbs that landed on the ground.

"How're we going to get this back to the kitchen?" Rowan asked.

"I have just the thing," I said, and went around the corner to bring back the trolley. "Ta-da," I sing-songed, as if I were a magician producing a white dove from a top hat.

"You're always prepared, aren't you?"

"I was a Boy Scout."

"You were?" Rowan looked genuinely surprised.

"You sound like you don't believe me." I gave her a lazy grin to show her I wasn't offended.

"I guess I see you as more of a free spirit."

There were worse ways to describe me. "I wasn't a Boy Scout for long," I confessed.

Rowan smirked at me. "I sense a story. What did you do? Sew grass seed where it shouldn't be?"

"I wish I'd thought of that at the time. No, my mom had an argument with the troop leader, and she never let me go back."

Rowan clapped a hand over her mouth, but the giggle escaped. "You got thrown out of the Boy Scouts because of your mother?"

I gave a long-suffering sigh. She didn't know the half of it. "Not just the Boy Scouts. Swimming lessons, Drivers Ed. You name it, I got thrown out of it, because of Mom. In the end I refuse to join anything else because I knew it would only be short-lived. That's why I ended up working with Dad in his business. He never allowed her near his clients."

Rowan burst out laughing. "I'm never going to see your mom in the same light again."

"The stories I could tell you," I intoned. "But not now or Charlie will have my hide."

"We'll save them for another time," Rowan said.

I pushed the trolley while Rowan picked up the throws and cushions. It would have been nice to have left them there, but as usual with an English summer, there was a promise of rain later, and Mom would kill me if her best cushions got damp and moldy.

I showed Rowan where the kitchen door was and took her in to meet Jo, the family cook. I heard Rowan inhale a deep breath as we walked in, and I realized she was bracing herself for another meeting.

I looked over my shoulder to give her a sympathetic smile. "It's okay. Jo doesn't normally eat people."

"And if I do, it's with a light Chianti and fava beans," Jo said sarcastically. She gave Rowan a frank look. "And this must be my new boss."

"That's yet to be decided," Rowan said, holding out her hand. "Rowan Mayfield. Good to meet you, Jo."

"Likewise, Ms. Mayfield," Jo said.

I really liked Jo and her husband Robin. They were in their forties, and both were children who grew up on the estate. Jo was a blunt, sarcastic, fire-breathing dragon in her domain, but she was fiercely loyal to the Mayfield family and loved her job. I could see she was wary about the newcomer. I decided to do a little intervention.

"Call her Rowan," I said. "She really doesn't like being called Ms. Mayfield and she isn't going to call you by your surname."

Jo nodded. "Understood. I hear you two are getting hitched."

I tried not to stiffen, so of course she caught my involuntary flinch. I really need to improve my poker skills.

"I told Robin it was rubbish," Jo crowed. "There's no way you have a girlfriend."

"Thanks," I said dryly. "You don't think someone like me can have a girlfriend?"

"Not one like Rowan, son." Jo looked Rowan up and down. "She's way above your league."

"That's not true," Rowan said, leaping in before I could defend myself. "Adam is amazing, funny, and honorable." She stopped as she realized we were both staring at her. "What?"

"I was teasing him," Jo said. "But I've realized he picked a good one here."

"I didn't pick her," I said somewhat defensively. "Rowan's not a bottle of wine."

Jo groaned and threw her hands up. "You're both as bad as each other. Well, if you're going to play fake fiancées then good luck to you. Just don't break his heart, okay?" She aimed the last at Rowan.

"I'm a big boy now, Jo. I can manage my own heart. Besides, I thought you were meant to grill her in private, instead of doing it in front of me."

Jo shrugged. "She'll only tell you anyway. I thought I'd save time and get it out in the open."

I swear I heard Rowan mutter something under her breath about England being full of crazy people, but I could have just imagined that.

I turned to Rowan. "Listen, I was going to invite you to meet my dad today, but—"

Rowan gave me a sympathetic nod. "It's okay, you don't want strangers in when he's had a bad night. There'll be another time."

I was grateful that she didn't seem offended. "I've got to go. Jo will point you in the direction of Willow."

I leaned in to kiss her cheek and then I was out the door before Jo could make another crack.

Chapter 13

Rowan

I wished Adam could have stayed by my side, but I knew he had work and he needed to spend time with his father that day. So I turned to Jo and smiled. "Where do I put the dirty plates and cutlery?"

"I'll deal with that," Jo said. "I know you'd be happy to do it, but nobody ever does it right, so I'd rather do it myself."

I wasn't about to trespass on someone else's domain or dishwasher. "Could you tell me where I can find Willow?"

"She's probably in her office this time of day. Come with me and I'll show you where it is."

Jo pulled the trolley out of my way, and I followed her out of the kitchen and across the hall. Willow's office was next to Harry's, I realized. I was pleased to be getting some sense of direction in the old house. Jo knocked on the door and waited until she heard a call to enter.

"Ms. Mayfield for you, Ms. Mayfield."

Jo turned and caught my glower. "Sorry, Rowan. I'll remember next time."

I thanked her because she was only following protocol and went into the office. I was struck by the difference between Willow's office and

Harry's. Harry's study was a place where he played and occasionally worked. Willows was a place where she worked and probably never played. It was a light, airy room with pale blue wallpaper decorated with small cherry blossom. Long cream drapes swept to the floor. But the room was full of filing cabinets and shelves full of heavy tomes and box files. Willow's desk was a functional item I would have expected to buy in IKEA, piled high with papers. I had obviously interrupted her morning's work.

Willow smiled at me from behind her desk. "Good morning, Rowan. Did you sleep all right?"

"I did, thank you." I hesitated. "I don't want to disturb you if you are working."

Willow gave her desk the side-eye. I could see that she was torn between doing her duty as a hostess and reducing the mountain of work on her desk.

"I can take myself round or find something else to do," I said hastily. "Or maybe Ash can do it."

"Ash is at the stables, and I'm busy with invoices, but maybe Raymond could take you. Harry is out this morning."

I hope I didn't look as horrified as I felt at the idea of my uncle who thought I was a tart show me around the house. Willow must have caught the look on my face because she gave me a wry smile.

"He's the best person to do the job. He knows more about the house than any of us," she admitted. "And it gives him a chance to apologize to you."

I gave a curt nod. It had to happen sometime. "Where is Raymond?"

"In his study waiting for my phone call."

"This is a setup, isn't it?" I asked suspiciously.

"Whatever gave you that idea?"

"Maybe because I'm not as stupid as I look."

Willow actually laughed at that. "Oh my dear, you are the last person I would say looks stupid. I've already warned Raymond to be on his guard before he gives the house away." I wasn't sure if Willow was being funny or sarcastic, or maybe both. But I felt a touch of smugness knowing they were wary about me. I would pass that on to Adam. I had to be careful though. This was their turf, not mine—yet. It was up to me to keep my defenses up.

"Just point me in the direction of his study," I suggested. "And don't make the phone call."

"I guess I owe you that."

"I guess you do," I agreed.

She got up from her desk and headed towards the door, stopping as she put her hand on the handle. Willow looked over his shoulder at me. "Don't be too hard on him."

"It was said in the heat of the moment. I understand."

Willow opened the door and pointed to the room directly across the hall. "That's Raymond's study."

I straightened my spine, squared my shoulders, and channeled my inner grandmother. She would have turned any man who insulted me into ground beef. I walked across the room and heard the snick of the door behind me as Willow returned to work. I knocked on the door and waited. I expected to hear a call to come in, but there was nothing. I raised my hand to knock again, and the door suddenly flung open. My uncle was lucky he didn't receive a punch to the nose.

"Oh!" Raymond took a step back, plainly flustered to see me standing there. "Rowan."

"That's right. Your niece, the tart."

I thrust out my hand. Raymond didn't make any effort to take it as he went bright red. In fact, I'm not sure he saw it. I felt a bit of an idiot standing there with my hand out. I let my hand fall and then suddenly he realized and grabbed it for the most awkward handshake. I sighed. This really wasn't going well.

"Let's start over," I suggested. "Hi, Raymond, I'm your new niece, Rowan."

Raymond took a moment to catch up, then he held out his hand. "Hi, Rowan, I'm the idiot who insulted you. I'm very sorry about that. It's really nice to meet you."

I had to give him points for trying. I took his hand, and we shook hands properly. He was a tall, slim man in his late fifties, a similar build to Harry, with a full head of almost white hair and bushy eyebrows. He looked like a younger version of William in the painting.

I got down to business. "I was hoping you'd be able to take me around the house this morning, as Willow is busy."

It was as if I'd flicked a switch inside him and

his whole face lit up.

"I'd love to," he said hastily. "But are you sure you're ready for this?"

I squinted at him. "You're not giving me the ten-cent tour then?"

Raymond looked horrified. "You need months, even years, to appreciate this house."

I wondered if Willow had thought this would be some form of torture for me. A way to put me off. What she didn't realize was that I loved history. My mother had loved history. My grandmother, she liked it too. I was going round this house for the two generations of women who'd been denied.

Raymond proved to be an entertaining tour guide. I realized Mayfield house had always been, first and foremost, a home. The architect's dream for the house had been to make it a castle but he'd run out of money, so the property stood vacant until it was snapped up by a businessman. Charles Mayfield had bought the property and the estate and set about making it one of the premier estates in England. Unusually for the time, not owned by a nobleman. But Mayfield had connections in the Royal Court and knew how to make himself useful. It turned out Mayfield knew how to keep his mouth shut. Scandals came and went but not a word passed Mayfield's lips. He stayed away from drama on his country estate, leaving generations of Mayfields to be born and die in peace in this comfortable house.

It was kind of sad to realize that the line would die out with the current generation. Even with five children, William Mayfield had had one grandchild, me, but no boys. I said that to Raymond who just shrugged.

"It's happened before. The Mayfield family is very good at bearing girls. But previous generations kept the Mayfield name and added it to the married name. The next generation dropped the married name."

"That way they kept the inheritance in the family?"

"Precisely."

I arched an eyebrow. "And you thought you do the same with me, but by marrying me off to a cousin?"

"Cousins can marry here although it's not recommended." He wrinkled his nose. "Inbreeding, you know. The toffs were always at it. Weakened the line."

"I'm not going to marry a cousin," I said firmly.

It was Raymond's turn to raise an eyebrow. "Of course not. You've already got yourself a fiancé, haven't you? You could do a lot worse than young Adam."

I looked at him in surprise. "You don't mind that he's one of your staff?"

"I'd be a hypocrite to complain," he said dryly.

I remembered what one of my aunts had said about Raymond being with someone on the estate last night. "You are friends with someone who works here?"

"I am," he said, but he didn't give me any further information, and it wasn't my business to ask.

"Do you know who the archivist is for the family?" I asked, seeking to change the subject.

Raymond looked surprised. "I am. I took over from a cousin who passed away last year. Why?"

I explained about the gardening journals, and he nodded.

"They're on the list, but Cousin Jeremy primarily focused on the house. He was only partway through when he died."

"I could help, if you want. I've had experience in my last job." I was pleased to see he looked thrilled and surprised by my offer. "I don't want to step on anyone else's toes."

"You won't be," he assured me. "I've been trying to get some of the lazy idiots who lived off my father to help but none of them lifted a finger. It would give you a chance to get to know the history of the estate."

A knot of tension eased in me. I had found a way into the family and for the first time I saw a glimmer of a future ahead of me if I stayed here.

As we walked down the stairs, Raymond said, "Willow will be pleased. She was always complaining that we'd lose the garden records one day if we didn't make an effort to archive them. I think she has visions of fire or flood or something."

I hesitated but then I said "Adam told me about the oral tradition of the gardeners. Not only passing information through the journals but discussing the information."

Raymond nodded. "A lot of the staff couldn't read or write so the oral tradition was essential."

"What about Adam's father? I know he's passed a lot of information onto his son, but maybe he would be able to be recorded talking about the garden. On good days," I added hastily, as I saw Raymond shoot me a look.

"It's a thought," Raymond agreed. "If he's well enough. I guess I thought most of the information had been passed to Adam but it's worth a conversation with the family. I'll do that soon."

Neither of us needed to speak the words that there was a limited timeframe to have this discussion.

We reached the bottom of the stairs in silence and Raymond patted my hand.

"Thank you for listening to an old man and for his accepting his lame apology."

"I was fascinated," I said sincerely. "I feel I won't learn everything I need to know in a lifetime, but today was a good start."

Raymond headed off to his study and left me in the hallway, not sure what to do with myself. It was still light outside and I decided to take a swift walk in the garden to see if I could find Adam. I had a lot of things to think about and I could really do with his clear head.

I walked through the kitchen. There were obvious signs of preparation for the evening meal, but the kitchen was empty. I would offer my services to Jo at some point. I was no cook, but I could chop vegetables with the best of them.

I stepped out into the late afternoon sunshine, blinking at the bright light, and wondered how I was going to find my pretend fiancé.

Chapter 14

Adam

Charlie let me sit with my father for a couple of hours in the afternoon to give my mother a break. I suggested she went out with a friend.

"The only place I'm going is my bed," she said, and walked wearily up the stairs.

I heard her bedroom door close. I made myself a coffee and went in to sit with Dad. He was sleeping peacefully after the visit from the hospice had increased his medication. The lines of pain in his face had eased. This was a cruel disease and there seemed no end. I was glad I was here for him and my mom.

I picked up the thriller I was reading, and sat in the armchair by the bed, preparing to keep a watchful vigil. The hero of the book was blowing up a railroad somewhere in the world — I'd lost track several chapters back – when my phone buzzed. I pulled it out hoping Charlie didn't need me already.

"Hey there, where are you?"

I grinned. Rowan must have finished her tour with Raymond. I discovered what she was doing when Willow came to find me. From the mischievous look on the woman's face she had set the whole thing up.

"Sitting with Dad. Where are you?"

"In the garden looking for you."

I wanted to go find her, but I couldn't leave my dad, and I knew neither of my parents could handle outsiders today.

"I can't leave here for a while. Mom needs to sleep. But we could go out for dinner?"

"I promise to have dinner with the family, but I'm sure they wouldn't mind if you joined us. You are my fiancé."

I grinned at the wink emoji. *"Love to. I should be free by six."*

"I'll clear it with Jo. See you later. I'm going to rest my blisters."

I knew Jo wouldn't mind cooking for me. The woman loved me after all. Pleased to have a plan for the evening, I went back to my thriller. I contemplated reading back to find out why they were blowing up the railroad but decided I didn't care enough. My thoughts kept straying to Rowan and looking forward to the evening in her company.

I walked over to the house rather than bringing the Honda. The evening sunshine was warm, and the heavy air was redolent with roses and honeysuckle. I saw a familiar figure as she leaned over the balcony. Her face was covered by her long, wavy, dark hair.

"Careful," I warned. "You don't want to fall over."

She stood, her face bright red but also grinning, and waved a dismissive hand. "It's okay, the gardener will catch me."

I folded my arms and looked up at her. "Oh? And who is this gardener? Should I be jealous of him?"

She grinned at me. "He's a sweetheart. He's taken care of me since I arrived here. You don't need to be jealous of him."

"Well, that's okay then. Have you had a good afternoon?"

"I spent most of it lying on my bed reading a book on the history of the Mayfield estate," Rowan confessed. "My feet couldn't take anything else. My blisters have gotten blisters."

I frowned, not happy to hear that she was in pain. "Do you need fresh bandages?"

Rowan shook her head. "Jo did first aid on them this afternoon. She said she didn't want me bleeding all over her clean kitchen."

I smirked because that sounded just like Jo. "Are you coming down or am I coming up?"

"Dinner's ready. They sent me to see if you were on your way, so I suggest I meet you in the kitchen."

"You don't want to hop over the balcony?"

She snorted. "Once a day is enough, Prince Charming."

I grinned at her. "See you in the kitchen."

I turned to follow the path around to the kitchen when she said, "You look very smart. No dirt on you."

My mother had insisted I dress up again for dinner in a dark-green button-down shirt and black pants. I was going to need to buy new clothes if this continued. My entire wardrobe consisted of T-shirts and shorts for working in the garden.

The kitchen smelled like heaven. I knew immediately that Jo had cooked my favorite dinner, cottage pie. Even my mother's cottage pie wasn't as good as Jo's, although I'd never tell her that. Jo was at the stovetop but looked over her shoulder as I came in.

"Eating my food again, hey, Carless?"

I walked over and gave her a kiss on the cheek. "You know how much I like your cooking."

"I do," she agreed. "Before you go home don't forget to collect two portions that are in the fridge for your parents."

"Thanks." I was a little choked up but I kissed her again. I knew when I looked in the fridge there'd be more than two portions. Jo always sent me home with food so that Mom could concentrate on my dad and didn't have to cook.

"Where's your girl?" Jo frowned. "I sent her to find you."

"She did find me."

Just then my girl walked in with Raymond and Harry, Willow and Ash hard on their heels. Rowan was deep in conversation with Harry while the rest of them were giving benevolent if exasperated looks. They had to be talking video games.

"I have no idea what you're talking about," Willow sighed as she slipped around them and headed for the table.

Rowan opened her mouth as if she were going to explain but Harry laid a hand on her arm.

"Don't bother, dear. Discussing video games with the rest of the family is completely pointless."

"He's right," Ash said. "None of us care."

"But it's fun," Rowan argued as she joined me by the table. "You can ride horses and slay dragons and save the heroine."

"You can ride horses for real," Ash pointed out.

"And you can slay the dragon in the family, and I saved the heroine," I murmured to Rowan. Her quick grin told me she'd gotten the message.

"You can talk about video games later," Jo said firmly. "Sit down and eat your dinner."

"Are you and Robin joining us?" Willow asked.

Jo shook her head. "Not tonight. We are going to meet friends. Just leave the dishes by the sink. I'll sort out the dishwasher later."

Rowan seemed set to argue again but I nudged her, and she subsided. The kitchen was Jo's domain.

"You look very smart, Adam," Harry said. He was wearing his usual button-down and dress pants which probably cost five times the price of mine, so it was kind of him to compliment me.

I saw Willow eyeing me speculatively. I wondered if she'd make a comment, but she just sat down and helped herself to the food.

Rowan and I sat next to each other. Her light perfume filled my senses and she pressed up close to me as she reached for the bowls of vegetables. This was our third evening meal together. I would be content to spend every evening of my life with this wonderful woman. I wondered if I'd said it out loud when she shot me a quick look, but I realized she was expecting an answer from me.

"I'm sorry, I was distracted. What did you say?"

She chuckled. "I said I hadn't realized we had Marisa Rosen's paintings in the house. Isn't she Greg's grandmother?"

"Yes, she is. I didn't realize the family had Marisa's paintings either."

"Your grandfather had a fondness for seascapes," Ash said. "There are two in your suite and one in what was William's study. William actually tried to buy paintings from Greg to complete the series, but Greg refused to sell."

"I think Greg is learning that he doesn't need to hang onto Marisa's paintings. He and Marisa have agreed that certain paintings can be sold for charitable use," I said.

"It helps when you have a rich girlfriend."

I scowled at Willow's acerbic remark because I knew it was aimed at me.

Rowan put her hand on my knee. "Greg could have been wealthy, but he put his love for his grandmother before his own needs. Now he's using the paintings for good."

I turned to her in surprise, and she blushed.

"I had a chat with Lily and Elsa this afternoon."

My girl had had a busy day.

Willow grumbled something under her breath, but she kept her peace. I was relieved. I didn't want to get into a fight with her about my friends. The sudden yelp Willow gave may have had something to do with it. Someone had kicked her ankle.

Dinner was a bit subdued until Ash started a

conversation about one of the horses. It never ceased to amaze me how animated she became when she was talking about the small stable of horses owned by the Mayfield estate.

"Do you own racehorses?" Rowan asked. There was a collective hiss around the table, and she stared at us wide-eyed. "What did I say?"

Ash rolled her eyes at her siblings. "They know I have a hatred of horse racing and many of the horses are rescues from the racing industry. But you weren't to know that."

"I do now," Rowan murmured. "Perhaps you could take me to meet your horses tomorrow?"

The hiss turned into a groan and Raymond gently knocked his head against the table. "She'll never let you leave."

"I'm not that bad," Ash protested.

I gazed in amazement as three middle-aged people pelted their sibling with pieces of carrot. Rowan wore the same bemused expression. "Don't let Jo catch you doing that."

"They can clear it up," Ash snapped, unimpressed. "Kids, all of them."

Then the four siblings grinned at each other.

"You must have been a nightmare as children," Rowan murmured.

"Me, Ash, and Raymond were," Willow agreed. "Harry not so much."

"That's because he spent all his time playing video games," Raymond muttered.

Harry threw his hands into the air. "What's wrong with video games?"

"Oh brother dearest, where can I start?" Willow

said.

Rowan just shook her head. Like me, she was an only child. I imagine she found the sibling bickering incomprehensible. But it was entertaining at least.

"Dinner and a show, what more could we want?" I murmured to her. Rowan chuckled and relaxed against me.

It occurred to me that Rowan had found her way of connecting with Ash, Harry, and Raymond. But how was she going to connect with Willow, who was arguably the most important member of the family? The one person who could force contesting the will. Willow was a workaholic, taking care of the estate. There had to be some way that Rowan could connect with her.

I watched Willow interact with her siblings, relaxed and happy, and then the way she glanced at Rowan, her eyebrows knit together. She still wasn't relaxed about Rowan's presence in her house. Willow caught me staring at her and her lips pursed together. I didn't want to make her the enemy, but would she be the one to prevent Rowan claiming her inheritance?

Chapter 15

Rowan

Four weeks later

I wrapped the throw around me and drew my knees up to my chest. It was peaceful here in the old folly. I looked out over the lake and watched a pair of swans gracefully circle the water. My phone buzzed periodically but I ignored it. I didn't want to be found. I knew it was cowardly, but I was hiding from everyone, including Adam. I'd grabbed a cushion and a throw and vanished to the folly to think—again.

I had a decision to make, and I had to make it soon. The only problem was I had no clue what my answer was going to be.

I shivered as the wind cut through me even through the throw. The temperature had dipped in the last week. It was hard to believe I'd been at the estate for four weeks and Fall was nipping at Summer's heels.

I had to decide whether I was staying or going. I couldn't make the family wait much longer. But now there were other considerations.

At least employment wasn't one of my concerns. I had no jobs to return to. I'd handed in my resignations when I decided to stay for a few weeks. But even if I did return for good, I'd have enough money to take my time and find a job I wanted to do.

For the first time in my life, I had money in my new UK bank account. I was learning what it was like to be a wealthy woman. For someone who'd never had a cent to her name, it was unnerving. I was also learning to drive on British roads and Adam made me drive him over the estate to get used to different vehicles. Driving was essential if I wasn't going to be trapped on the estate.

I had to return to Boston soon. The lease was almost up, and I needed to clear out my apartment. Adam had suggested sending in removers and transferring everything to a storage facility, but I had little enough to call my own. I didn't want to take the risk of losing precious memories of my family. Lily and Greg had offered to help but this was something I had to do by myself.

But the reason I was hiding here was the big decision. Was I going to stay or go? I didn't know. I really didn't know.

Over the past month I'd worked as hard as I ever had in my life, learning about the estate and the people. I'd made friends with my aunts and uncles, and even one or two of the cousins who'd approached me about living on the estate. There were still rumblings from the distant cousins about contesting the will, but with my aunts and uncles backing me, it quickly became clear they didn't have a leg to stand on. The days of handouts were over. If the cousins wanted to stay on the estate, they had to pay rent or work.

Willow, Ash, Raymond, and Harry had all separately and together asked me what I wanted to do. But the fact was I didn't have an answer. If I was going to stay here, I'd have to apply for residency. My lawyer assured me that it wouldn't be an issue, just a long process, and I was happy to let him worry about that. But until it was settled, I'd have to fly backward and forward to Boston.

I still had to decide if I was ready to become Rowan Mayfield, matriarch of the Mayfield family. If I flew back to Boston I'd be on my own again. Here I had Adam and his family. And for the second time in my life, I had a family of my own. I had an estate of people who wanted to get to know me. And I also had friends. Friends on the estate like Barry and Alfie, and two women who were dying to meet me. At least when I returned to Boston I could meet Lily and Elsa.

There was one other problem.

And he was starting to hurt.

I'd never have stayed the course without him by my side. It was Adam who introduced me to everyone, who showed me I could be part of the Mayfield family. I hadn't spent a day apart from him. We shared breakfasts, lunches, and dinners. I was part of his family as he had become part of mine. I'd finally gotten to meet his dad, Simon, and I adored him.

Yet, Adam and I hadn't kissed beyond brief pecks on the lips. We held hands, he hugged me. I knew he was falling in love with me, and I couldn't deny my own feelings for him.

Adam wanted me to stay. I wanted to stay with him. But I wanted more than that. I wanted our fake engagement to be real. After one month I couldn't imagine my life without him.

But I also knew I had to stay for the right reasons. If I went home with money in my pocket, it would be easy to restart my life again, but I'd leave him behind. He couldn't just drop everything with his father so ill.

I groaned into my hands. I was going around in circles. Why couldn't I just make a decision?

"Here," Adam said.

I looked up to see him holding two travel cups. "Coffee?" I asked hopefully.

"Hot chocolate. Mom made it. You must be cold by now."

He handed me one of the cups and sat down next to me, pressing his warm body against mine.

"I won't be able to hide out here much longer," I admitted. "It's getting too cold."

"You have an entire house to hide in," he pointed out, not bothering to hide his grin. "Your suite, for instance. No one would expect to find you there."

It had become a standing joke that I spent as little time as possible in William's suite. I'd done nothing to the rooms since I arrived. I slept there. I showered there. But apart from purchasing new clothes, it was the same as the day I moved in. I couldn't do anything to make the suite mine until I made that decision.

But there was another reason I claimed the folly as my hidey-hole. Here, Adam would find me. He wouldn't go in the house without an invitation.

I sipped the hot chocolate, letting the warmth spread through me. We sat there in peaceful silence, and I wondered what it would be like, to return home and not see this man every day. He'd become such a part of my life, it hadn't occurred to me what it would be like when he wasn't there.

"So why are you hiding?"

"I needed to think."

Adam grunted. He didn't ask me if I'd made a decision. He knew I'd been wandering around in circles for the past two weeks.

"I might have an answer," he said.

I turned to look at him and noticed the tightness in his expression. "Oh?"

"Dad saw the oncologist today."

Usually Adam told me if he was going to be tied up with medical appointments. How had I missed this? "What did the oncologist say?"

Adam smiled and his expression softened. "He's doing really well. They thought he wouldn't last the summer, but with the last round of chemo, they've extended his prognosis."

"That's great news."

"It's good news," he said, tempering my enthusiasm. "He might have another Christmas with us."

"That's good," I said. I took one of his hands in both of mine, trying to give him comfort.

Adam brushed his warm lips over my knuckles, sending a shiver through me. "The thing is, I need to go back to Boston. Dad has asked for something that's at my apartment. And I could get it sent here, but I thought as you needed to go, maybe we could travel together."

"You and me?"

"I wasn't thinking about inviting Harry or Willow," he said with some amusement.

I nudged him with my elbow, and we scuffled for a moment or two. I would miss this. The fun. Just being together.

"I was planning to meet Lily and Elsa while I was in Boston."

"That sounds like a great idea. I can't wait to see Greg again. I wish we had time to visit the animal sanctuary."

"Isn't that in Texas?" I asked.

I hadn't spoken to Elsa's husband, Davy, but I knew his family ran an animal sanctuary on their farm.

"It is, but I'm not sure I'll have time to do that as well. The thing is, Rowan, my Dad's only got a short period where he's going to be feeling better and Mom can cope without me. I need to go soon. And I know you need to sort out your apartment."

Tension butterflies set up in my stomach. This wasn't just a maybe. Adam had a fixed schedule. "When are you thinking we should fly?"

"Elsa is sending her jet. It's capable of international travel. It'll be here tomorrow."

My jaw dropped open. "Tomorrow? We're flying by private jet?"

Adam gave me a wry smile. "There are benefits to having wealthy friends. I looked at getting flights but when I mentioned it to Greg, the next thing I know Elsa is sending her jet. She's like that. You'll soon learn."

I ran my hand through my hair. I really should have stayed hidden. This was all too much.

Adam took my hands in his and turned so that I had to look at him. "I know that you're nervous and returning home makes it all real for you." The man knew me better than I knew myself. "But we don't have to be gone for long."

I looked at our joined hands. "I didn't want to return home by myself. But I knew you couldn't come because of your father. That's one of the reasons I've been hesitating."

Adam let out a sigh of relief. "I had no idea how you'd react. It's a relief to know you're not going to scream at me or throw me in the pond."

"Like I'd do that. So just how big is this jet?"

Chapter 16

Adam

The jet was bigger and more luxurious than I'd ever seen.

Rowan was as wide-eyed as me. She glanced my way as we entered the cabin. "Which seat do you want?"

"Why pick just one?" I quipped.

The cabin seemed to stretch on forever, with a long couch opposite a huge TV.

I felt as intimidated as Rowan looked. I was a gardener. She was a receptionist. Neither of us belonged in this world.

I made jokes about having wealthy friends, but they were thousands of miles away. The Mayfield family lived quietly on the estate. They had wealth beyond my imagining, but I didn't notice it.

From the chauffeur driven car that had picked us up to the private airport where security was quick and polite, this was luxury in our faces.

A young man who'd introduced himself as our flight attendant smiled at us. "Take a seat, Mr. Carless, Ms. Mayfield. The pilot says we're cleared for take-off."

We nodded like puppets and slunk into leather seats opposite each other. We declined an offer of drinks, and the flight attendant vanished with a polite smile.

"I can't believe I'm going home in a private jet," Rowan said, looking out the window as the jet engines started.

"How did you fly here?" I knew Rowan wouldn't have had the money for the flight.

"They sent me a ticket to get here. Economy," she murmured.

"What a surprise."

"It's the first time I've been out of the country. I had to get a passport."

"How did you like the flight?"

"I hated every minute of it," Rowan confessed. "I was stuck between two men and one of them thought he could hit on me for the whole flight. The other one needed a shower." She blinked. "Did you just growl?"

I'd been unable to hold back the growl in my throat. "I hate the thought of a man harassing you. Sitting next to the pretty girl is no reason to not take no for an answer."

Rowan's eyes widened. "You think I'm pretty?"

"Now you're fishing."

Rowan grinned. "Maybe a little."

"Yes, you're pretty, and no, he shouldn't have hit on you."

"Don't worry. I made it plain I didn't want anything to do with him." Her glee was obvious.

"Uh-oh. What did you do?"

"After the fourth time his hand wandered onto my thigh, I told him if he did it again, I would scream at the top of my voice. I assured him I had good lungs. He kept his hands to himself after that."

"Would you have screamed?"

Rowan nodded. "I don't like men who harass women either. Sometimes they need a lesson in respect."

There wasn't much I could say to that except a murmured, "Agreed."

But then we were taking off and I looked out of the window as the ground fell away. My stomach gave a small lurch as we launched into the morning sunshine. I saw Rowan relax and realized she'd been holding her breath until we were in the sky.

"How's your Dad?" Rowan asked.

"He's fuming because he didn't get to go in the private jet." I smirked as I remembered his grumbles. "He didn't quit complaining all evening."

"And your Mom?"

"She's fine. Did you know Harry has offered to sit with Dad every afternoon to give Mom a break?"

Rowan nodded. "I knew he was gonna ask Allyson. He didn't want to intrude while your Dad was so sick."

"Mom's so grateful for the support. Jo sent her a week's worth of cooked meals. Mom grumbled that she wasn't incapable of cooking for herself, then burst into tears over the foil cartons."

"You know Willow is desperate to help in some way?"

I grimaced. "I think that might be a step too far for my mom. I told her Willow called me a gold digger and Mom went ballistic."

Rowan chuckled. "Poor Willow."

"Hey, she was rude about me," I protested.

"She wanted to marry me off to an actual gold digger," Rowan pointed out.

"True, true. Do you know which cousin she had in mind?"

"Willow won't say, and the others are keeping quiet. But one or two of the cousins have invited me out to dinner. I'm thinking about it."

My jaw dropped. "But we're engaged." Then I saw her lips twitch. "Rowan Mayfield, you're a wicked, wicked woman."

"I certainly hope so," she said cheerfully.

I shook my head but I couldn't deny Rowan made me laugh.

The flight went on. It was wonderful to have someone on hand to serve drinks, snacks, and meals. But it was still endless. Rowan and I watched movies on the TV. She curled into my side on the long couch and after a while, I realized she'd fallen asleep.

"There's a bedroom at the back," the flight attendant said when he noticed Rowan had dozed off.

"I don't want to wake her," I admitted. I was comfortable with Rowan nestled into my shoulder and the movie had enough explosions to keep me entertained. If I got bored, I had another thriller in my pack, which the flight attendant had placed within my reach.

I watched the movie until my yawns had gotten ridiculous. Then I rested my head back on the couch. Maybe I could take a short nap too.

"Wakey, wakey, Adam."

Someone shook my arm. Annoyed at having my sleep disturbed I cracked open one eye. "Wha—"

Rowan smiled down at me, her brown eyes twinkling. "Time to wake up. We're going to land soon."

I groaned as I sat up, running my hands through my hair.

"Are you always so grumpy when you wake up?" she asked innocently.

I glowered at her. I couldn't actually say anything as I'd said the same to her. "That coffee better be for me."

Rowan grinned at me and handed me the cup. "Like I'd deprive you of coffee."

I yawned, grimacing when my jaw cracked painfully. "How long was I asleep?"

"No idea. I woke up an hour ago and the end credits were rolling." She tugged one leg under her and picked up her own cup. "I spoke to Lily. We've got an offer to stay at her condo."

"That's kind of her."

"She and Greg are already there."

"Where do you want to stay?" I asked. I wasn't sure whether Rowan wanted to stay in her own apartment or not.

"Let's stay with them tonight. I'm dying to meet them. We can stay at my apartment tomorrow."

"Okay." I squinted at her. "Are you sure that's

what you want?"

"No." Rowan expelled a breath. "I don't know what I want."

I ran my hand down her silky hair. "Are you worried if you stay at your apartment, you'll never want to leave?"

"Something like that," she confessed, leaning into my touch. "But my landlord has someone waiting for the apartment, so staying there for good isn't an option."

"But it's your place," I suggested. "Familiar."

"Mine." Rowan huffed. "Not mine for much longer."

"You have to split your time between here and the UK. Why don't we look for another apartment while we're here?"

"That's a good idea. I could at least decide which area I want to live in." She squinted at me. "Why are you so excited?"

"I've never gone apartment hunting," I said. "I lived with Mom and Dad and stayed in the apartment when they left."

Rowan nodded. "Same with me. I've lived in the apartment my entire life."

"I guess I just moved from living with Mom and Dad to living with Mom and Dad."

"What will happen when you move back here?"

I swallowed my cooling coffee. "Mom wants a small place of her own, so I'll look for a apartment for me."

"Will you start your business again?"

"Greg has offered me a job. He's spending more time traveling with Lily than he expected.

He needs an assistant. We're gonna talk about it while we're here."

Rowan tilted her head as she regarded me. "You didn't tell me that."

I could see the hurt in her expression. "He asked me yesterday."

"Is that what you want?"

I shrugged. "I don't know. I'm not sure about working for one of my best friends, even Greg, who's more like me than me. But I know I need a job until Mom and I settle."

Rowan patted my knee. "You do what's right for you and Allyson. You know I'll help."

I laced my fingers with hers as it rested on my thigh, a gesture that had become familiar to us. I hoped one day I could kiss her.

As we walked down the stairs of the plane, I saw a luxury car and a couple waiting beside it.

I nudged Rowan. "That's Greg and Lily." A tremble ran through her, and I took her hand. "Lily is sweet and kind, I promise." I knew Greg wasn't the problem, but meeting Lily Duchamp, even if they had become friends on the phone, was a big deal for Rowan. "I won't leave you."

"Promise."

"I promise."

We walked over to them. I saw Lily clutch at Greg's hand and wondered if Rowan had noticed it. Lily was shy too and she was probably just as nervous as Rowan.

I grinned at Greg. "You should be working."

He grabbed my hand, pulled me into a bear

hug, and thumped my back. "So should you."

I stepped back, turned to introduce Rowan, and discovered she and Lily were hugging each other.

Greg caught my eye and winked. I grinned at him. It was a relief to both of us that our girls were fine.

He thumped my shoulder. "Let's go home. You must be tired."

"We slept most of the way," I confessed.

"On the couch?" Greg queried as if he knew.

"Yeah. One minute I was watching a movie. The next, Rowan's shaking me and telling me we'll be landing soon."

"It happens to me every time," he admitted. "Traveling privately is something else."

Rowan and Lily had disentangled from each other. Lily was a few inches shorter than Rowan, with strawberry-blonde hair and huge blue eyes. Greg had fallen in love with her the moment Lily had landed in his arms. I held out my arms and Lily hugged me tight.

"Thank you for taking care of Rowan," I whispered in her ear.

She leaned back and looked up at me. "Thank *you*, Adam. Thanks to you, I have a new friend."

I knew she wasn't just saying that. Lily had been born into a privileged world, but friends had been thin on the ground until she met Greg.

Then Greg held out his hand to Rowan. "Good to meet you, Rowan."

"I've heard so much about you." Rowan held out her hand, but he gave her a quick hug.

"All of it lies, I assure you," Greg said.

I raised an eyebrow. "What about the time you got locked in the barn and had to climb out through a hole in the roof?"

Greg huffed and we all laughed.

Then we piled into the car, and Rowan settled next to me. She stared out of the window as we drove through the city.

"All right?" I murmured.

"It's only five weeks since I left. It feels like a lifetime ago," she said.

Had it only been just over a month? I felt as if I'd known Rowan forever.

Chapter 17

Rowan

I closed my eyes and let the hot water relax my tired muscles. I'd almost cried when Lily had shown me the bathroom and told me to take my time. The shower was wonderful after the long journey. Even in the luxurious plane I still felt grimy after traveling. I could have stayed in there for hours, but finally I turned off the water and wrapped myself in the soft white towel.

Once I was dressed in a clean blouse and jeans, I left my bedroom and went in search of the others. I could hear muted talking in Lily and Greg's room. Adam and I had a guest bedroom each. Lily apologized for how small they were. I didn't say that the guest bedroom was almost the same size as my old apartment. I didn't want to make her feel bad.

I wasn't surprised to find Adam staring out of the large windows at the activity going on in the port. It was dusk now and the lights were slowly illuminating the city. The condo was lovely, with endless windows and stunning views. I'd never been in a place like it. My old apartment looked out over dumpsters and an alley. As Greg had been brought up two blocks away, I imagined his outlook had been similar to mine. I wasn't surprised he was mesmerized by the view.

"It's breathtaking, isn't it?" I murmured.

Adam put his arm around my shoulders. "You're going to find this strange, but I really miss the view over the valley, and the roses in my parents' backyard. I guess I've gotten used to the English countryside."

I thought about it for a while. Every morning I rolled out of bed to stare at the fields and woodland over the valley. The leaves were just starting to change as fall approached. I would miss that view if I returned to Boston full-time.

"How are you guys doing?" Lily asked behind us.

I turned to smile at her. "Enjoying the view."

She gave it a dismissive wave. "After living at Holly Cottage, this is nothing."

I felt the gulf between her life and mine open up. Normally Lily was very careful not to wave her privileged life in my face but right this moment I was feeling it. I also understood this was my problem, not hers, and if we were to stay friends, I needed to get over it.

Greg coughed and she blushed. "I'm sorry, I didn't mean—."

"It's okay," I assured her quickly. "In my head, I'm still living in my apartment, and working two jobs."

"I feel the same," Greg told me. "I've been with Lily for two years now and it still seems like a fairytale."

"You know that's really sappy, don't you?" Adam said to him.

"Like you're any different," Greg scoffed. Then

he yelped as Lily elbowed him in the ribs. "That hurt."

She hugged him close and reached up for a kiss. "I'm sorry."

It was sweet how he melted at her touch.

Adam put his arm around me, and the four of us stood watching the outside world for a while longer.

Elle and Davy joined us for dinner. It was one of Davy's rare trips into Boston.

"I'm not a city boy," he confided, almost shyly. "But I wanted to meet you."

"Where's your boy?" I asked, disappointed not to have a chance to cuddle their son.

Elle grimaced. "He's with Greg's sister. Skip is teething and really grouchy. I didn't want to take him on the plane in case he felt worse. That's why it's just a fleeting visit. We're going home early tomorrow morning."

I was disappointed but I understood. Elle was delightful and so down-to-earth. I could see why she and Davy fitted together. They both wore scuffed working boots just as Adam had said. I still had to pinch myself that I sat next to two of the richest women on the east coast and they wanted to be my friend.

If it hadn't been for Adam, I'd never have met them. He caught my eye and smiled at me. I wondered how he'd feel if I asked him to kiss me.

"You really like Adam, don't you?" Elle murmured.

"Is it that obvious?"

From the twin eye rolls from both girls, I guessed that it was.

"I think it's mutual," Lily assured me. "Greg says he never stops talking about you."

Warmth spread through me. I really hoped so because I wasn't sure my heart could take it if he walked away.

"How are you doing now you're back here?" Lily asked me.

"I don't know yet," I confessed. "Ask me tomorrow."

Wearily, I sat in my apartment looking at the boxes in front of me. "Is this my life? A dozen boxes represents my entire life?"

Adam was spaced out on the couch, his eyes closed. He'd worked like a Trojan. I don't think I could have done it without him. "You did give most of your things to Goodwill," he pointed out.

At Lily's suggestion, I'd paired my belongings down to the bare minimum so I could take it back on the plane. Elle had offered us the Ralston plane home if we weren't fussy about the exact day. We willingly agreed, and when we settled on a date, Charlie had agreed to meet us at the airport in the UK, with the Mayfield truck to transport the boxes.

It was weird that I had very little I wanted to keep. I agreed with the landlord to leave the furniture behind so he could rent it furnished to the next tenant. This left me with clothes, books and games, and memories of my mom and Gran. I didn't even need all my clothes as I'd replaced them over the last four weeks. Most of my wardrobe had gone to Goodwill too. The Converses and Doc Martens were coming with me though. I'd missed those. I slipped the Doc Martens on like greeting an old friend.

Greg was due any minute with his old pickup. We would just have enough room to pack the boxes. One of the boxes belonged to Adam. He'd opened the box to show me three old journals belonging to his great-great-grandfather, the original gardener in the family. His dad wanted to look at the journals one last time. They were stunning in their delicate illustrations and discussion on seeds and planting.

"Is there anything else you need to bring back?" I asked.

Adam sat up and ran his hands through his hair. I wanted to smooth out the tousled mess. His hair always started neat at the beginning of the day but by the end it was every which way.

"I don't think so. Most of my gear is back home. I kept a few things in Greg's apartment, but I only need this box."

I looked around the apartment, checking that I hadn't left anything that I wanted to take with me. It was strange. I expected to be more upset or depressed about the fact I was leaving, but instead it was almost a relief. This one decision was out of my hands. When I came back – if I came back – it wouldn't be to here.

Adam hauled himself to his feet at the knock at the door. He looked through the peephole and then opened it. Greg walked in, looking around with obvious curiosity.

"Are you ready?" he asked.

"All packed," I agreed. I pointed to the stack in the center of the room. I expected him to make some remark, but he just nodded and picked up a box.

"Adam and I can take these while you stay with the pickup," Greg suggested.

"These are the journals," Adam said. "This box goes in the cab."

Greg's eyes lit up. "I can't wait to look at them."

I spent the previous night listening to the two of them discussing botanical websites with Elle. I'd told Adam bluntly he could never laugh at me for playing video games. He was as big a nerd as I was. He tsked at me and declared "Never," but he knew I was in the right. I'd waggled my eyebrows at Greg to tell him he was also a nerd. He groaned and sought sanctuary in Lily's arms. Lily had just patted his head and told him she loved him, which was all he seemed to need.

"Where are we going to store the boxes?" I asked.

"At Ralston House," Greg said. "And Elle will arrange for them to be taken to the plane when you fly back."

I felt tears prick the back of my eyes. Everyone was so good to me. Then Adam pulled me into a hug. I draped my arms loosely around his waist and rested my head on his chest.

"I've done what I came to do," I said to the people around the dining table. "That's it. My life in that apartment is over."

I was sad, but I still felt that sense of relief. It was time to move on.

"You'll need a place to stay as you'll be flying in and out of Boston," Lily said.

"I do," I agreed. "I don't know how long it will take to arrange the visa. I've left it in the hands of Mr. Roberts. Thank you, by the way. He's been amazing."

"Elle had nothing but good things to say about him," Lily agreed. "The reason I'm asking is that a condo next to ours will be vacant soon."

"I can't afford that," I said, horrified at the thought.

Adam held my hand. "You need to remember who you are now, Rowan. You can afford to buy a condo here."

"I don't even know if I'm going to stay at Mayfield," I whispered.

Our gazes locked and I could see the pain in his eyes. He didn't want me to leave. But I couldn't commit. Not yet.

"Now you've completed the work on your apartment, why don't you spend a few days with Marisa?" Greg suggested, diverting my attention. "You'd be away from the city but not at Mayfield. I find being by the ocean gives me a chance to think."

"No, I couldn't disturb your grandmother," I protested. "Besides, Adam needs to get back for his dad."

The one thing I had learned since meeting Greg was how much he loved his Gran. They had a cottage near hers which Greg had intended to use for research. But he'd confessed that it was harder to focus on his work now he was married to Lily. They spent a lot of time traveling over the country looking at nonprofit organizations who could benefit from Elle and Lily's foundation. I understood now why Greg needed an assistant.

"Actually," Adam began, "Mom suggested we spent more time here as Dad is doing well." He blushed. "I think she wants me to talk to you about the job, Greg, and start looking for an apartment. If you'd like to spend a few days by the ocean, Rowan, why don't we go? It's probably just what you need to clear your head.

I had that boxed-in feeling again. Much as I loved Adam and his friends, they were always organizing me, and it was starting to feel stifling. I looked up to see Lily studying me closely.

"What do you want to do, Rowan?" she asked softly.

I barked out a laugh. As if I had any idea. "I want to hide away in my apartment and never come out."

Lily nodded. "I used to feel like that every time my parents organized my life."

"I haven't had control of my life since the second I opened that envelope from my grandfather's lawyers."

"Take a few days away," Lily suggested. "Adam can look at Greg's plans, and you can take your time to think about what you really want."

I glanced at Adam and caught him studying me just as hard. "What do you think?"

"I could really do with a few days of sea air and Marisa's cooking," he confessed.

"Is her cooking that good?"

"Gran's the best cook in the world," Greg said.

"There's nothing like Marisa's cooking," Lily agreed.

Adam gave a vehement nod, "You haven't lived until you've tried Marisa's food."

I held my hands up. "Okay, okay. We're going to Maine." I furrowed my brow. "How are we getting there?"

Chapter 18

Adam

I was happy to drive to Maine as I'd driven the journey before with Greg. But Lily insisted I took her driver and car. She confided in me that Ronan desperately wanted to see Marisa but always needed the order. I wasn't quite sure what she meant but it was nice to be chauffeur driven.

Her driver/bodyguard, Ronan, scared the living daylights out of me. I was tall, but he was huge and bulky, with a grim face. I swear the guy could pummel me into a pretzel. I knew from past discussion that Greg felt the same way. Ronan was very protective about Lily. He'd been her protection detail since she was a small child and even now you could see how hard it was for him to stand down and let Greg take care of her.

I expected Rowan to be just as intimidated by him. But Rowan took one look at the bodyguard and was charmed from the first moment they met. And the feeling seemed to be mutual.

"Why does he never smile at me like that?" Greg muttered in my ear.

"Maybe because you're not a pretty girl?" I suggested.

Greg looked at me as if I'd offended him. Then he shoved me, and we scuffled for a few minutes.

When we stopped Ronan was scowling at us and the girls were giving us looks of amused exasperation.

I'd expected we would stay at Greg and Lily's place, Holly Cottage, but Marisa loved having guests, so we were staying there. I was worried that Rowan would find that awkward as she didn't know Marisa, but Elle and Lily had done a lot to assure her that Greg's grandmother was lovely. She knew I adored Marisa too.

We had left the city limits behind when she said, "I don't care where I am as long as I'm with you."

I brushed the back of her knuckles with my lips. "You couldn't have said anything to make me happier."

I knew at some point we'd have to discuss our relationship, but there were so many other things to think about. Rowan's future, my father's illness. We could end up with Rowan staying at the Mayfield estate and me moving back to Boston. Sometimes I lay in bed at night, and everything was scrambling around in my head. No wonder Rowan was so tied up in knots about everything.

As usual, Rowan passed out on my shoulder partway through the journey. I held her close and looked out of the window at the passing scenery. I was so distracted by my own thoughts I almost missed when we turned off the highway for the drive down to Lavender Cottage.

I kissed the top of Rowan's head. "Rowan?"

She grumbled and settled herself more comfortably against my chest.

"It's time to wake up, sweetheart. We're nearly here."

She gave a long sigh, which was kind of adorable, and sat up. Rowan yawned once, then ran her hands through her hair, wincing when she got caught in a tangle.

"I guess I fell asleep again, huh?"

"Yes, you did. Do you always fall asleep when you're traveling?"

"I never really traveled anywhere before." She looked out of the window. "Where are we?"

"We're almost at Lavender Cottage," Ronan said from the front.

I saw the moment that Rowan spotted the ocean.

"Oh wow," she gasped.

I smiled at her enthusiasm. To be honest I was just as excited myself. I didn't get to visit the ocean nearly enough. Mayfield Estate was deep in the English countryside and there was nothing like the vast American coastline to inspire awe.

Greg's grandmother waited for us by the gate as we pulled up. I don't know how she knew when people were arriving, but she always waited to greet them. The last time I saw her was at Lily and Greg's wedding. Then she was very much Marisa Rosen, renowned artist. Now she was dressed in a light sweater and jeans, her long silver hair tumbling around her shoulders.

Rowan grasped my hand and I saw the panic in her eyes. "I know nothing about art," she said hurriedly.

"What do you think about Harry's paintings?" I

asked.

Her brows furrowed as if she was confused by my sudden question. "I like them. They suit the house. Why?"

"Look at the paintings in the cottage."

I kissed her cheek and then got out of the car. Ronan opened Rowan's door for her which I could see unnerved her, but she thanked Ronan for his courtesy.

She held onto my hand as we walked over to Marisa who beamed at us.

"It's been too long since I saw you here, Adam. And Rowan, it's lovely to meet you. Greg and Lily are always talking about you." She looked over my shoulder and I noticed her cheeks went a little pink as she met Ronan's gaze. Interesting. I would have to quiz Greg on this. "Ronan, good to see you. Are you staying for dinner?"

"I am," Ronan rumbled. He'd have to drive back that night because Lily had an event tomorrow, but he hadn't objected to the round trip in one day.

As Marisa took Rowan into the cottage, I went to follow with our packs.

"Ms. Mayfield is lovely," Ronan said as he shut the car door.

He couldn't have said anything that would have made me smile brighter. "She is. I'm so lucky to have met her. But call her Rowan or she'll get all grouchy."

"Noted."

Ronan surprised me by putting a hand on my shoulder before we went into the cottage.

I frowned. "What's wrong?"

Ronan put his hands in his pockets. "I was worried when you asked Lily and Elsa for help. I don't like people who take advantage of them."

"You know I'm Greg's friend?" I pointed out.

"I do, but that didn't mean to say I had to trust you."

Now I was irritated. "You know who Rowan is? A Mayfield?"

His expression didn't change. "I do now."

I nodded in understanding. "You checked her out."

"I checked out both of you."

I folded my arms across my chest and regarded him flatly. "And what did you discover?"

"That you gave up your life and business in Boston to help take care of your father and took over his job."

"What of it?" I knew I sounded unfriendly, but I didn't care.

Ronan didn't seem fazed by my anger. "It says a lot about your character."

"And Rowan? Not that it's any business of yours."

"If it involves Lily, it *is* my business. Ms. Mayfield has worked hard all her life and now she's been offered the impossible dream." Ronan looked at the cottage. "I know how that feels. But she also returned Lily and Elsa's money, so I'm not worried about her taking advantage of them."

"But?" There was always a but.

"What do you get out of Rowan staying at the Mayfield Estate?"

I gave him a thin smile. "I get the woman I love."

I stalked into the cottage, leaving him standing there. He needed to butt out before I helped him to. It was a ridiculous thought. Ronan could squash me with one finger. But it made me feel better, nevertheless.

I found Rowan and Marisa on the deck looking out over the sea. I smiled at Marisa. "This is new since I was last here." I indicated the decking.

Marisa smiled at me. "My old bones needed something more comfortable than the beach."

"You will never be old," I assured her. It wasn't fake flattery. Marisa would go on forever.

"I thought you'd run away," Rowan said, a slight frown between her eyes.

"Ronan wanted a word." Rowan nodded, but I caught Marisa's knowing look. "I expected to find you running along the beach," I said to Rowan, changing the subject. "Rowan's always been a city girl, Marisa. Now she has to live with lots of countryside."

"She can enjoy the ocean while she's here," Marisa said.

Rowan held out her hand. "I was waiting for you. If that's okay with you, Marisa?" she added hastily.

"Of course it is, Rowan. You could probably do with the stretch after that long journey."

"I fell asleep," Rowan confessed. "Adam thinks I fall asleep whenever we travel."

"That's because you do," I pointed out.

Marisa chuckled. "I used to do that to. Now I

don't go anywhere, and I fall asleep to the sound of the waves."

"That sounds blissful," Rowan admitted.

I heard Ronan coming through the kitchen, so I took Rowan down the steps onto the beach. It wasn't much of a beach in terms of sand. But it was interesting with driftwood and sea glass and interesting pebbles. Greg and I had spent many hours combing the beach. Some of my found treasures were still in my bedroom at home.

"Are you going to tell me what got you so angry?" Rowan asked.

I huffed out a breath. "How did you know?"

"The last time I saw you that angry was when you discovered Raymond had called me a tart."

"Ronan was concerned that we were taking advantage of Lily and Elle when we asked them for help, so he investigated both of us."

"That's understandable," Rowan said. She sounded so mild I shot her a look. "He's there to protect Lily, Adam. I'm not surprised he checked us out."

I shoved my hands in my pockets and stared at the waves gently crashing on the beach. "I hate the idea of people prying into my business."

Rowan burst out laughing. "Seriously? That's all anybody's done to me for the past four weeks. And you said yourself William knew exactly where I was. He was probably spying on me for years."

"So you think I'm being ridiculous?"

Rowan nudged me. "A little. Ronan was just doing his job. Leave it at that."

"You have a kind heart," I said.

She wrapped her arms around my waist, so of course I had to put my arms around her shoulders. We stood for long moments, staring out to sea.

"I could stay like this forever," she whispered.

"On the beach?" I asked.

Rowan pulled back to look at me. "In your arms."

Chapter 19

Rowan

We had an early dinner as Ronan needed to return to the city. My friends were right. Marisa's cooking was outstanding. Between Ash, Jo, Allyson, and Marisa, surely one of them could teach me to cook more than toast?

Adam gave me a hug when I said that. "We'll put it on the things-to-do list."

After dinner, Adam vanished into the den to call his mom, and I called Mayfield House to keep them apprised of my plans. Robin answered and handed me over to Harry.

"You're staying with Marisa Rosen?" Harry sighed like a teenage girl. "I'm such a fan."

"I promise to introduce you at some point," I said.

From his excitement I could have been offering him the world.

When I returned to the kitchen, Ronan was nowhere to be seen and Marisa was reading a book.

"Ronan's left already," she said.

"He has a long drive." I didn't say it, but I was relieved. Adam was still seething over Ronan's conversation with him. "My uncle is envious that I got to meet you. He's a painter."

She nodded. "Henry Mayfield? Oh yes, I've seen some of his work. We'll have to talk."

My uncle would swallow his tongue. He really would.

"Where's Adam?" I asked.

"He's on the beach. I think he had some thinking to do."

"Is he all right?" I asked, worried about him. "Is it his Dad?"

"He's fine," Marisa assured me. "Adam's just like Greg. He goes to commune with the world when he needs to think."

I looked out onto the beach, seeing a lone figure. "I'll go check he's all right."

"It's blustery now," she warned.

When I went out onto the decking, I found Adam on the beach, staring out at the rough waves. He wore a thick-knit sweater and old denims cut off to make shorts. He didn't seem to be bothered about the pebbles as he stood barefoot on the beach or notice the light rain that soaked into his dark hair. He was obviously lost in thought, and I was loathe to disturb him. But then he turned and saw me, and his whole face lit up. He liked me. I had to keep reminding myself of this and hug it to my heart.

Blinking against the rain blowing in my face, I picked my way down the steps, not wanting to slip and fall. I'd done enough to embarrass myself since I'd known him. The beach was more pebbles than sand and I was glad I'd put my sneakers on.

Adam smiled at me as I joined him. "It's gotten windy."

I sucked in a lungful of tangy, salty air. "It smells good."

"It's wonderful here," Adam agreed. "No wonder Greg never wants to leave."

"According to Lily, he's the same when he reaches Black Feather Farm. I think he just likes open spaces."

Adam looked out to sea. "He's not the only one."

I wasn't really a beach girl myself, but I'd only been to a beach vacation once when Mom had gotten a summer job on Cape Cod. I'd been young, maybe eight or nine, and I'd been allowed to run wild for the summer. It had been hard to return home with all the restrictions of city life. But I'd soon gotten used to it again.

"It's so wild compared to Mayfield," he said.

I could barely hear him above the crash of the waves. "Mayfield is so open to me compared to the area around my apartment block."

"It's all relative, I guess. Mom used to hate the green lawns when we moved to Mayfield. She said if the Good Lord had intended her to live surrounded by grass, He'd have made her a cow." Adam snorted. "Now she thinks He has a point. The grass is lovely as long as she doesn't have to mow it."

I have a wistful smile. "Your mom would have loved my mom. She was a city gal. She showed me pictures of Mayfield once. She said "All that space for one miserable family. It should have been razed to the ground and apartment blocks for the poor put in its place."

"And now you've been there?" Adam asked.

I thought about it rather than giving him a trite answer. "I think Mayfield has its place, just like Lavender Cottage. And Mom would have loved it, even if she refused to admit it."

He nodded, seeming pleased with my answer. "I've gotten used to the peace at Mayfield. I like going out at sunrise and listening to the birds and the delicate scents of the flowers."

"My gardener is a poet," I said without thinking.

He raised an eyebrow. "Your gardener, huh?"

"Well, according to the will, you are my gardener," I quipped.

"Well done, Ms. Mayfield, you dug yourself out of that hole."

Adam smirked at me, and I chuckled.

"I thought I did well."

He bent to whisper in my ear, and I instinctively leaned in close. "I like the idea of being your poet."

Our smiles faded and we locked gazes, ignoring the wind and rain. I liked the idea of him being my poet too, and not just my fake boyfriend.

"Let's go for a walk," he suggested.

It was better than us staring awkwardly at each other, so I nodded, and we wandered along the cove.

"Marisa said Greg collects driftwood for her when he's here," I said. "There's a basket by the kitchen door. Did you know Marisa makes bowls?"

"I do. I've been here before, remember?" He laughed down at me, but it was a gentle tease rather than mocking laughter.

I'd been the focus of people's humor before, and it wasn't pleasant. This was soft and I didn't bristle—much.

"She tried to teach me to make a bowl, but I was useless," Adam admitted. "My creativity is only in the garden."

I nodded. "I'm not creative at all. Strictly practical. Just like my Mom."

"Your Aunt Willow is a fine watercolor painter, but she'd never admit it. There are a few of her paintings around the house. She talks about Harry being the family artist but never mentions herself."

"How come this is the first time I've heard this?" I asked.

Adam blinked, light droplets of water on his lashes. "I just thought about it."

Before I had a chance to respond, the rain turned from a drizzle into a deluge and in seconds we were soaked through to the skin.

"Wild is one thing. Soaking wet is another," Adam said. He held out his hand. "Let's go back inside."

We ran up the stoop and into the kitchen. Closing the door on the noise outside made the silence almost deafening. Then the rain lashed against the glass and my hearing returned to normal.

Marisa handed us both towels. "Welcome to the rain."

"It rains in England, but this was something else," Adam said as he towel-dried his hair.

I chuckled. "It was fun."

"You have a strange idea of fun." He shook himself like a dog shaking its wet coat.

"Adam," I protested, hands up in a futile gesture to stop the water spraying me.

"You two are as bad as Greg and Lily," Marisa chuckled. "Now get out of your wet clothes and come back to the kitchen for hot chocolate."

I stripped out of my sweater and jeans as quickly as possible and into the only other change of clothes I had, another sweater in a pale green, and gray sweatpants. I brought my clothes down with me, hoping there was somewhere I could dry them.

Adam was already there, holding a large cup of chocolate. He grinned as he saw the clothes. "I did the same thing."

Marisa took them out of my hands and went into the laundry room. "Sit down at the table, dear."

I sat in the seat next to Adam and inhaled the sweet aroma of hot chocolate. "That smells good."

"It tastes even better," Adam assured me.

I sipped at the hot chocolate and discovered he was right. The taste was amazing. "There's something...a bite to it."

"Chili," Marisa said, returning from the laundry room. "I've always added chili to my hot chocolate.

"It's the best I've ever had," I said sincerely.

She beamed at me. "You picked a good one, Adam. Make sure you keep her."

"I think she picked me," Adam said.

I smirked at him over the rim of my cup. "It was you or the shark. You were the safest option."

He placed a hand over his heart. "Safe? You think I'm safe? I'm wounded."

"He's very melodramatic, isn't he?" I said to Marisa.

"I think you might have to dial that down, Adam," Marisa said, not bothering to hide her amusement. "You don't want to scare Rowan away."

He waved a dismissive hand. "Nothing could scare Rowan. She's invincible. She's a superhero."

Adam barely knew me. It was his absolute confidence in me that was overwhelming. No one had ever felt that way about me except my mom. He made me melt.

I caught Marisa's expression out of the corner of my eye. She had that satisfied expression that I never trusted. Then she saw me watching her and grinned.

"And what's Adam's superhero power?" she asked.

"The strength to see beyond the ordinary," I said softly. "He made me look at my new family and my grandfather's bequest and asked me to dive deeper into what my Grandfather had given me."

Adam stared at me and then he smiled. "I did, didn't I."

"I would never have walked around the estate if it hadn't been for you. Or talk to Harry and Willow. I would never have had the confidence to make friends with Greg and Lily, Elle and Davy.

And you, Marisa. You opened your home to me, a stranger, because Adam asked you to."

Marisa shrugged. "He loves you. That was good enough for me."

My jaw dropped.

"Marisa!" Adam sounded strangled.

"Did I say something wrong?" she asked, all wide-eyed.

"No, but you just can't come out it with like that. What if it's too soon?"

"It's not," I said quickly. "Too soon, I mean. It's not too soon."

"I think that's my cue to leave." Marisa groaned as she got to her feet. "Getting old is a real pain in the bones, my dears. I think I'll have an early night. Good night."

"Night, Marisa," I said.

Adam rose to kiss her on the cheek. "Good night."

Marisa kissed him and shuffled out of the kitchen, leaving Adam and I avoiding each other's gaze.

Adam huffed. "Grandmothers."

"Mine was just the same."

"You've gotten another one now. Marisa adopts everyone. Hey, it's stopped raining. Do you want to look at the stars?"

"I'd love to," I said.

I stepped out onto the decking and inhaled the post-rain ozone tang.

"Come with me," Adam said. "Away from the lights from the cottage."

He held out his hand and I took it. We walked

further down the beach. The tide was out now, the waves little more than a gentle murmur. The wind had died down to barely ruffling our hair.

"I can understand why Marisa never moved away from here," I murmured. "It's perfect."

"I hope you get a chance to think."

"I don't need the beach to think," I admitted. "I just need to face up to reality and move on."

"Where is home, Rowan?"

"Boston." I said that without hesitation. "And Mayfield. Boston is my home and has been my entire life. But I think I'd like to become part of Mayfield. You told me to learn about it and I have. It's a beautiful place, and there's so much I don't know."

"Do you think you could be the matriarch of the Mayfield clan now?"

"Oh yes," I said fervently.

Adam chuckled. "I think you could too. Look how much you've achieved just in a few weeks."

He was right. I'd come a long way from the frightened and angry woman who ran from the will reading.

"Staying in England doesn't have to be forever if it doesn't work," he continued. "No one's gonna think less of you if you hand over the reins to someone else."

I gave him the side-eye, because come on, had he met my new family?

His lips twitched. "Okay, maybe they will, but what does that matter? You don't have to care. The point is, and we discussed this before, you've got options now."

I sighed and stared up at the night sky. The stars were the brightest I'd ever seen. Even at Mayfield.

"It's so beautiful," I murmured.

Adam wrapped his arms around me. I leaned back against his solid frame. "Look up at the stars, Rowan. You see the same stars in Mayfield. It's a small world. Home is where you make it."

Home was in Adam's arms. I just didn't have the courage to tell him that.

Chapter 20

Adam

I woke about six a.m., feeling relaxed in head and body for the first time since I'd gotten off the plane. We had one last day at Lavender Cottage. I was ready to go home tomorrow, but I knew we were both reluctant to leave this place.

When Greg had suggested prolonging our visit, I'd been unsure. It had been hard to leave my mom alone to take care of my dad. If it hadn't been for Harry's offer to spend time with my father, I'm not sure I'd have agreed. But the peace and open space, and Marisa's gentle hospitality, had been good for both of us. I'd seen the strain ease from Rowan's face over the past three days and the tension in my muscles drained away, leaving me like a limp noodle.

We'd come here to help Rowan make a decision. After our talk under the star-lit sky, I'm not sure she was any closer to deciding her future, but I woke, knowing one thing to be true. I would follow Rowan Mayfield to the ends of the earth if she'd let me.

I didn't want to go back to sleep, and I felt too restless to stay in bed, so I got up and dressed in T-shirt and shorts and sneakers and headed to the beach for a run before breakfast. I ran the hard-packed sand along the water's edge, the length of the cove and back. Sand and water splashed up my legs as I pounded along the beach. It had been a long time since I'd gone for a run just for fun.

A solitary figure waited for me by the sea. I ran up to her, knowing my face was bright red, and my hair stuck up everywhere.

"You're up early," Rowan teased.

"It was late for me," I pointed out. "You're the one that's up early."

She pouted, then burst into peals of laughter, startling two seagulls. They squawked, scolding her and then took off, wheeling around for one last chiding squawk, before flying away.

"I think you upset them," I said, grinning at her.

"I'll apologize when they come back," she said solemnly.

"How will you know which seagulls to say sorry to?"

"They'll be the ones yelling at me," she said, like it was obvious.

I snorted and she grinned at me. I loved this. I loved the fact we could tease each other. I'd never had such a relaxed relationship with anyone before.

"Breakfast is ready," Rowan said, "and there's a surprise."

"What is it?" I was suspicious, never too keen on surprises, since the day in fourth grade when Danny Campbell handed me a wrapped box on my birthday, and I opened it to discover a huge spider. I screamed and ran away. I'd never been allowed to forget it throughout school.

"You'll like this one," Rowan said. She knew my reservations. I'd confided this story on one of our trips around the estate. It turned out we both hated spiders.

We walked hand-in-hand up the stoop and into the kitchen.

And there was my surprise.

Not a hairy spider.

Greg and Lily wore matching grins and matching sweaters.

"You need a shower, buddy," Greg said. "You're wearing the beach."

"You guys dressing the same now?" I retorted.

"My gran made these for us," he said.

I turned to Marisa to apologize, but she smirked at me. "The other gran."

"Gotcha!" Greg crowed.

"You're a—" I started.

"Yes, he is," Rowan interrupted hastily, "but before you get into more trouble, why don't you shower?"

"You need hosing off first," Greg said. "I'll do that."

I looked down at myself and groaned. Greg was right. I was more sand than anything else. I kicked off my sneakers and socks and placed them by the door. Yep, I needed to hose down before I covered the cottage in sand.

"I'll do it," Rowan said, her serious expression spoiled by a giggle.

I sighed. Whoever hosed me, it was going to be cold and unpleasant.

Rowan followed me out onto the decking, and I

pointed to the coiled green hose.

"Do your worst," I said.

Rowan looked far too gleeful as she picked up the hose. The blast of water she aimed at me was as horrible as I anticipated. I gasped and spluttered as I took a mouthful of water.

"Sorry," she cooed.

I growled and she laughed, but she turned the hose on my legs and away from my face. It didn't take long to wash away the sand but by the time she finished I was as cold as a popsicle.

"All done," Rowan said brightly and turned off the water.

I shivered so hard, my teeth chattered. "Sure you didn't miss a bit?"

She waggled the hose and I shut up.

"Here," Marisa said from the doorway, holding out a towel. "Dry off then you can have a shower."

The towel was warm and welcome. I dried off, then I was allowed back in the kitchen. Greg had disappeared but Lily was on the phone. She mouthed "Elle. Charity." Then she returned to her conversation.

I scurried away to get showered and dressed, hoping by the time I returned, there would be coffee and breakfast as promised.

Ten minutes later I was warm, in fresh clothes, and heading for the kitchen. I met Greg coming back into the cottage.

"Hey, you look better," he said.

I noticed Greg's tense expression. "Is everything okay?"

Greg nodded. "Just talking to Davy about an

extension to the animal sanctuary."

I hadn't gotten to the farm because of my dad, but I'd seen the photos and Greg had taken me on a virtual tour. "I thought the extension had the greenlight."

"It does, but Griff and Robyn are concerned they've taken on too much. Davy's already working the farm and the sanctuary. They need staff rather than relying on volunteers. Although the volunteers are wonderful. Have I told you about Miles's dad?"

I knew Miles was one of the first dogs at the sanctuary and he'd been adopted by a vet. But I furrowed my brow. Wasn't Elle one of the richest women in the country? Couldn't she fund a staff member or three?

Greg caught my expression. "I know what you're thinking. It's just getting past Davy's pride."

I understood. Davy had had to swallow his pride in a big way simply by being with Elle, by accepting help from the Ralston family.

Greg gave him a wry smile. "We're all working on him gently. He has a family who loves him."

"I have faith in you guys."

"I can't wait to get you there," Greg said, clapping my shoulder.

"Me too. When my Dad..."

Greg squeezed my shoulder. "I get it."

I swallowed hard and headed into the kitchen. Rowan looked at me, her smile fading when she saw my expression. I smiled at her, and her sunny expression returned.

"I thought you'd gotten lost," she said.

"It was Greg's fault," I said, throwing him under the bus without a second's hesitation. "He talks too much."

I really deserved the shove he gave me.

Marisa ignored the scuffling between us. To be fair, she'd seen it before. Greg and I couldn't help behaving like kids when we were together.

"Wash up quickly and sit down at the table."

Greg and I grinned at each other and went to wash our hands. Then I sat next to Rowan.

Marisa brought out huge, fluffy omelets and hot, strong coffee. It was exactly what I needed after the run, especially with the warm and just baked bread straight from the oven.

Lily groaned after her second piece of toast. "I'll never get into my dress now."

Rowan furrowed her brow. "What dress? Aren't you already married?"

"We are. It's for a gala. I promised Diana I would go with her," Lily said. "It's a beautiful dress and Valerie's already had to let it out once."

I saw Rowan's confusion. This was a world she wasn't part of yet. "Diana is Lily's mom," I said, "and Valerie is her dress designer. She's Greg's sister."

"Wow," Rowan managed. "Valerie Crenshaw is your sister?"

Greg nodded. "One of my big sisters. You know her?"

"I know *of* her," she said. "My mom used to read fashion magazines."

"She's just my really annoying big sister," Greg assured her.

"Don't be mean about your sister," Marisa said, "even if she was really annoying to you."

That was Greg's cue to launch into all the woeful tales of how mean his siblings had been to him. As he sat with three only children of course we lapped it up, even though I'd heard most of them before and had participated in some of the stories. But I'd have to thank Greg because by the end of his stories, Rowan was laughing again, and she'd stopped feeling inadequate. I touched her hand under the table and she laced her fingers in mine.

"We've got to get back to work," Lily murmured, "but would you like to come over for dinner?"

"I've already prepared dinner," Marisa said. "You come here."

Greg would never say no to Marisa, so they arranged to have dinner and watch the sunset. I didn't care where I was if I was with Rowan.

Rowan sat with me while I called Mom to check on my father. I breathed a sigh of relief when she greeted me with a cheery hello, and I saw Rowan's immediate smile.

"Is everything all right?" I asked.

"Dad's fine. He and Harry are chatting about the old days. I've been banned from disturbing them. You know what your father is like when he gets talking."

"I know. I'll be home in a couple of days."

"I know, hun. Take care. Give Rowan a kiss."

And she was gone, leaving me shaking my head.

"I don't think they even know that I've gone."

Rowan laughed and rested her head on my shoulder. "They know. They just want you to have a good time."

I pressed a kiss to the top of her head. "That's from my mom."

I heard her happy sigh. We sat like that for a few minutes, then I looked outside. It was a lovely day still. "Want to collect sea glass?"

"Love to," she agreed immediately. "What's sea glass?"

I needed to remember that my girl had rarely been out of the city until she took a plane halfway across the world to a country estate in England.

"I'll show you." I stood and hauled Rowan to her feet. No one could stay at Lavender Cottage and not collect sea glass.

We tugged sweaters over our heads because the breeze was still fresh and headed out of the cottage with Marisa's old wicker basket.

I showed her the pieces of glass, battered by the waves into pebbles. The blues and greens, yellows, and sometimes mauves, all sparkling in the sunlight.

Rowan picked up a red pebble and held it up to look through. "These were from bottles?"

"Most of them."

"They're beautiful," she said, sounding awed. She touched a light blue one with one fingertip. "I wish I knew where they came from. You said Greg collects them for Marisa?"

"He does. She says she finds it hard to bend for any length of time, but I think she knows he loves combing the beach for things Marisa can use in her sculptures."

"They really adore each other."

"They do. She loves Lily too, and Lily soaks up her love like a sponge."

Rowan squinted at me. "That's an odd thing to say."

I sought for a way to explain. "Lily comes from a different world from us. Even Elle had more of a life like ours. Lily has always been isolated from friends. Marisa welcomed Lily into her family without even thinking about it, just like she did with you. Greg loves her. And she's got friends like Elle and Davy. And now you and me."

Rowan seemed to think about it. She turned the red sea glass in her fingers over and over. "I used to hate girls like Lily. Rich, beautiful. Dressed in clothes I'd never be able to afford in a lifetime."

"You've met Davy and you'll meet his sister, Robyn. You should get them to tell you about the gala dinner." I took her chin in my hand and turned her to face me. "I haven't got two cents to rub together. Does that bother you?"

Her smile was sweet. "You gave me a family, Adam. I don't care about what's in your bank account."

Chapter 21

Rowan

While Adam did a few chores for Marisa, I did what everyone had been telling me to and went for a walk along the beach by myself. I found a large, smooth rock at the far end of the cove and sat down to look out over the rolling waves.

Maybe I'd be handed an answer to all my problems. Or maybe I'd just end up stiff and cold. But it was beautiful here. Wild and untamed, a sharp contrast to the formal elegance of Mayfield.

I would be going home tomorrow. And that thought startled me more than anything else. Even in my head, I called Mayfield my home. I would be going home to a country that wasn't mine, to live with a family I still barely knew, in a place that was completely alien to me.

Yet I wanted to be there. Somehow the people and the house in the middle of the English countryside had gotten under my skin. I still didn't know what I was doing, and I wasn't sure I was fully accepted, but I wanted to go back there.

I turned to look at the cottage at the far end of the cove. I wasn't sure if I saw a figure moving on the decking. I squinted and it looked like Adam. He was the other reason I wanted to go back. There was no point trying to deny it any longer. I loved Adam Carless. He was about to face the most difficult time in his life, and I wanted to be by his side. But did he want me there? It was time that I gathered up my courage and asked him.

I started a slow walk back to the cottage. The colors were so bright. The blues and greens of the ocean. The sharp blue of the sky. It almost hurt my eyes. Sunlight glinted on the sea glass on the beach. I picked up a few more pebbles for Marisa's collection, but when I found an emerald-green piece that reminded me of the greens of Mayfield, I slipped that one into my pocket. I'd give that to Adam's father so he could look at it and feel close to the gardens he'd tended.

I was halfway along the cove when I saw a familiar figure loping towards me. His grin when he realized I'd spotted him made my heart sing. We met in front of Holly Cottage, Greg and Lily's place.

"I thought you'd gotten lost," Adam said.

"Were you worried about me?" I teased.

He put his finger and thumb together with maybe half an inch gap between them. "A little," he allowed.

"Have you done everything Marisa asked you to do?"

"I have. I thought we could go say hello to Greg and Lily. Greg wants to talk to me more about the job offer and Lily says if you join us, you could have a group chat with Elle."

I loved the idea of being able to talk to my friends. I couldn't think of a better way to spend my afternoon.

Several hours later we had decamped to the beach to watch the sunset while we ate dinner. Greg and Adam had started a fire in the fire pit on the beach. We ate fresh fish cooked by Marisa as the logs crackled and hissed.

As we sat on the beach, Adam's arm around me, I watched the sky turn from blue to pink clouds to streaks of orange and red. Finally it seemed the whole sky was a blaze of oranges and reds.

"You have a beautiful display for your last night, Rowan," Marisa said.

"I've never seen a sunset like this," I murmured.

Adam held me closer. "I have, and every time I forget just how magical it is. I think in the city we're so busy, we lose sight of how amazing the sun rising or setting can be.

"I was too busy trying to get to and from work to worry about a sunrise or sunset," I admitted.

"The colors tonight remind me of Lily's dress the first time I met her," Greg said.

Lily smiled at him sweetly. "You're right, sweetheart. It's almost exactly the same color." There was a pause. "At least it was until you covered it in dirt."

Greg and Adam both groaned.

"We're gardeners," Greg explained. "We're always covered in earth."

"Don't I know it." Lily winked at me.

Adam obviously decided to change the subject. "The sunrises and sunsets are beautiful at Mayfield, but even so, most of the time I'm working so I don't take time to appreciate it...and

Rowan is usually asleep." It was his turn to wink at my outraged expression.

We sat in silence after that, watching the vivid display. The sun slipped behind Lavender Cottage, leaving streaks of orange and red in the distance, until they too were gone, and the faint sprinkling of stars became visible in the night sky.

Marisa sighed and smiled at all of us. "I'm thinking s'mores. What do you think?"

Like any of us were going to turn that down.

I lost track of time, but at some point in the evening Marisa got to her feet with a shaky groan. "I'm done, my dears. See you in the morning."

"You have to look your best," Greg said with a mischievous grin. "Ronan will be here to collect us."

Marisa smiled at him serenely and walked up the stoop and into the cottage.

"She knows better than to engage me," Greg said, his smile turning wry.

"You shouldn't tease your grandmother like that," Lily chided. "Or Ronan. You really shouldn't tease Ronan."

Greg looked at her as if she were stupid. "I don't have a death wish. I'd never tease Ronan – much."

"What's going on between your bodyguard and Greg's grandmother?" Adam asked.

I was anxious to hear the answer too.

Lily huffed at our curious expressions. "Like they would tell me."

"So there is something going on between

them," Adam repeated.

"I think they like each other," Lily said.

I was expecting Greg and Adam to laugh at her tame description, but instead they both nodded as if they totally understood.

"It's good to find someone who's a friend," Adam said, and I didn't miss the look he sent my way.

There was an awkward silence for a few minutes, then Lily turned to me. "Have you made any decisions about your future?"

I pressed my lips together. "Do you know the one thing that keeps going around in my head?"

They shook their heads in unison.

I took a deep breath. "What does a little receptionist from Boston know about running a multi-million-dollar estate in England?"

Lily tilted her head. "Do you know that Elle ended up in much the same position as you? Her grandfather gave her the family industries, over her father."

I nodded because Elle had told me the story. I think she'd been trying to make me feel better.

"There was a point when she nearly had a breakdown, trying to do too much. In her mind she had to be responsible for absolutely everything, when she had no clue what she was doing."

I knew just how she felt.

"It was Davy, from the little farm in Texas, who pointed out the solution to the problem."

"What did he say?"

"She needed to ask the right people. She'd been

so busy trying to do everything herself, she forgot there were experienced people running the industries who could help her. When she picked up the phone, she found they'd been waiting for her call."

I knew Lily was trying to tell me something, but I felt like I was missing the point. I turned to Adam who took my hand and smiled at me.

"What Lily is saying is that you don't have to do everything yourself. You have an estate full of experienced people who are waiting for you to ask them for help. And that includes your aunts and uncles. Willow is dying for you to ask for help. When you respect their experience, they know you respect them. They don't expect a little receptionist from Boston to know what to do. What they want is that receptionist to acknowledge that they have that experience. Mayfield is a team."

I stared at him, then I groaned. I thought I'd been listening to the people on the estate. Had I really been that oblivious? I needed to have serious conversations when I returned to Mayfield.

We stayed out on the beach for another hour, talking about Greg's plans for his research. I didn't know much about gardening, but I did have a keen interest in history, and his knowledge of plants over the centuries in Boston was fascinating. He turned to me at one point and apologized for his enthusiasm.

"Never apologize," I assured him. "It's fascinating."

When that conversation had ended, Greg produced a small radio from inside the cottage. He held out his hand to Lily and it was sweet to see the way she melted into his arms. It was as if they were the only two people on the beach.

Adam looked at me hopefully. "Ms. Mayfield, could I interest you in a dance?"

"I'd love to," I said eagerly.

He enfolded me in his arms, my head resting in the crook of his neck, our joined hands over his heart. One dance melded into two and I lost track, content to be in his arms.

We danced for a long time, until I looked around and noticed we'd been left alone on the beach. Greg and Lily had vanished, and it was just Adam and me, under a billion stars.

Adam snorted as he realized the same thing. "I guess they were trying to be tactful."

"It was nice of them," I agreed.

"Rowan."

There was a strange tone in his voice, and I turned to look at him. "Is everything all right?"

Adam took my hands. "Rowan, I know I haven't got any right to ask you this."

My heart started fluttering at what he was about to say. Did he want me to release him from our fake engagement? It wasn't like anyone believed we were really engaged anyway. They all knew it for the maneuver it had actually been.

"Please don't walk away from me... Mayfield."

I let out the breath I didn't even know I was holding. "I won't walk away," I promised, and it was a promise to him as well as my family.

"You mean that?" Adam sounded like he was still holding his breath, as if he expected me to change my mind.

"I wouldn't say it if I didn't mean it," I grumbled. Then I nudged him to show I wasn't being serious.

"You don't know how happy you made me."

"I made the decision to stay earlier today. If the family agree then I'm staying. I just need to tell them." I grimaced, not looking forward to having that conversation. It wasn't that I thought my aunts and uncles would be a problem, but there were still those distant cousins threatening to take me to court.

"If you have Willow on your side, everyone else will fall into line," Adam said.

"I thought I had to get the estate on my side," I reminded him.

"You did, which is why Willow has your back now."

I thought about that for a long while. "Adam, I want to be here for you too. I know you need to focus on your parents. But I want you to know that I'll be by your side the whole time."

After a hoarse "thank you," Adam hauled me into his arms and we stayed silent under the stars listening to the snap and crackle as the fire died down, and the whoosh of the distant waves.

I would miss this when I went home, but it was time to plan my future.

Chapter 22

Adam

Four weeks later

The gentle knock at the door early one morning surprised me. I looked at my mom who was still in her pink pajamas as she roused herself over morning coffee.

"Are you expecting anyone?" I asked, then crammed toast into my mouth.

"The carers are due at eight," she said. "Chew before you answer the door."

I looked at the clock. It was only just after seven, and the carers never turned up early. I usually returned home for breakfast and left as they arrived. I swallowed my toast and opened the front door.

Not the carers.

I couldn't stop my ear-to-ear smile at the sight of Rowan. I hadn't seen her for over a week because she'd been away in London taking care of business.

I enfolded her in my arms. "You didn't tell me you were coming home," I scolded.

"I wanted it to be a surprise." Her voice was muffled as her face was buried in my sweater.

"It's the best surprise ever."

I picked her up and twirled her around, enjoying her startled squawk.

"Put me down," she ordered.

I did as she asked and smiled down at her. "What time did you arrive back?"

"About three minutes ago. I met Charlie who told me you were having breakfast."

The fact that she'd come straight to see me rather than heading for a much-needed sleep made me so happy.

"Let the girl come in," my mom scolded. "Thank goodness you're back, Rowan. He's not quit sulking since you left."

"That's not true," I protested. But from the expressions of the two women in my life it was a waste of breath. I hadn't been sulking. Moping, maybe. I missed Rowan so much.

"Is Simon awake?" Rowan asked.

I opened the door and poked my head around but closed it quickly when I heard Dad snoring. "Not yet."

Dad's health had taken a turn for the worse. We knew it was going to happen, but we'd hoped we'd have a little more time. He told us he was determined to hang on until Christmas. Mom contemplated having Christmas early. When Dad had heard about that he hit the roof. It had been a long time since I'd seen him so angry. He was going to have another Christmas with the family on December 25 just like everyone else. With that energy inside him I had no doubt he would be with us.

Rowan looked disappointed, but she said she

would see him later. I loved how much she enjoyed spending time with him, and since she'd presented him with the green sea glass, Dad hadn't let us move it from his nightstand.

"Come have breakfast with us," Mom said. "You know Simon always wants to look pretty for you."

It had become a standing joke in the family that Dad always made sure his hair was combed and he was wearing fresh pajamas when Rowan visited with him. My mom grumbled that he never made the effort for her, but Dad and I wisely kept our mouths shut.

I poured Rowan a cup of coffee and sat down opposite her. Mom fussed around the stovetop, cooking a full breakfast despite Rowan's protestations that she would be happy with toast. We both knew Mom wouldn't listen to a single word Rowan said.

"How did the business meetings go?" I asked.

It was easy to see the tiredness in her eyes and I knew from her increasingly terse responses that she'd found the week difficult.

"Thank goodness for Willow and Raymond," she said. "They slapped down the cousins who were trying to contest the will. Mr. Fox-William and Mr. Roberts have made it plain to them that contesting the will would be a really stupid thing to do, but I may have to find space on the estate for them. They want to live in the house rent-free. That ain't gonna happen." Her words got more and more snappy and her eyes indignant.

I wished I'd been at her side as she delivered that response to the hangers-on.

"Willow and Raymond are starting to push for us to set a date," Rowan muttered.

I choked on my coffee. "You're joking?"

"Nope. As far as they're concerned it's time for us to put up or shut up." She furrowed her brow. "At least I think that's what they said."

"That sounds like Willow." And I knew where Willow led, Raymond would follow.

Mom came over with a plate which she put in front of Rowan. "I thought they knew this was a fake engagement."

"We've never actually said it is or it isn't," Rowan murmured, before she dived into the bacon and eggs and toast.

"I think the lack of a ring gives it away," Mom said.

"So why are they pushing you for a date?" I asked.

"Because they can?" Rowan muttered around a mouthful of bacon. She chewed and swallowed before she continued. "I think they feel getting married would give me legitimacy and stop some of the cousins trying to make a claim."

"They're talking out of their—"

"Adam!" My mom didn't like any cursing in the family.

I shut my mouth with a snap.

Rowan gave me a quick sympathetic glance. "I agree with you, and I don't want to be pushed into anything just because the family wants it. That was the problem in the first place."

I looked away for a moment. I'd been looking for the right time to have this conversation with

Rowan, but since we returned from Maine, we had both been working all hours. Rowan had launched herself into learning the business of the estate and additional properties, and I'd been working with my team to tidy up the garden for winter and help my mom with my father.

I caught Mom giving me a 'get on with it" look, but I gave her a brief shake of the head. Now wasn't the time. Rowan had just driven through the night and what she needed was sleep.

Rowan sat back in the seat with a satisfied sigh. "Thanks, Allyson, that was amazing. I did have another reason for coming here." She flashed a smile at me. "I bought a new car."

"Don't you have enough cars?" I grumbled. The estate had at least ten cars she could use at any one time.

"I bought this one for me."

She waggled the key fob at me. What was I going to do? I loved cars.

We grabbed our jackets, and she took me outside. I took one look at the car and my jaw dropped open at the red monster.

"You bought a Mustang Shelby GT500."

"Yes, I did." Rowan grinned at me triumphantly.

"But why?"

"Because I wanted to do something really really foolish. Something I've never managed to do. Spend money just for the sake of spending it." She flashed a grin at me. "Want to drive it?"

I could stand there staring at it or I could drive the car. Stupid question. Of course I was gonna drive the car.

In the cold morning air, the engine roared into life. "You barely go above thirty miles an hour," I muttered. "Why have you bought this?"

"Live a little," Rowan laughed.

I gave a nod. I could do that. We both yelled in excitement as I gave the gas pedal a tap.

Rowan grinned at me. "I told Charlie you'd be late to work this morning."

"I really love my new boss," I said.

We drove away, and if there was anyone asleep in the row of cottages, they certainly weren't by the time we reached the end of the road.

After the excitement of the Mustang, which by the end of the day had been driven by every man on the estate, we had to get back to reality. I needed to have this discussion with Rowan about our future together. It couldn't wait any longer.

Two days later, I decided the best way of talking to Rowan was to take her for a horse ride through the estate. To my surprise Rowan had taken to horseback riding like a duck to water. My riding skills were competent rather than professional, but we had taken a few rides together under Ash's supervision. This time I asked Ash if Rowan and I could have a short ride by ourselves as I wanted to talk to her about our engagement. Ash's eyes grew comically wide, and she readily agreed with the caveat that we stayed on the estate. I understood that and was happy to saddle up two horses.

Rowan sighed in contentment as we ambled up

the track that led to the north end of the estate. There was a wide bridleway around Mayfield which was open to the public, but few riders knew about it, and William had taken efforts to keep it that way. He had never tried to block the path, he just didn't encourage people to use it.

"I really need this," Rowan said with another happy sigh. "I thought I was never going to get out of the office yesterday. I think Willow was determined to go through every invoice for the last five years."

"You really need to get yourself an assistant like Justin," I suggested.

Justin was Elle's assistant and possibly the most organized person in the universe.

"I don't think that I'll ever find an assistant as good as him," Rowan laughed. "He's the anomaly."

"I think you might have a point."

Rowan glanced over to me. "Are you going to tell me why you took me out for a horseback ride away from everyone?"

"What makes you think—"

"Because I know you," Rowan said calmly.

"Rowan," I started. "I want to talk to you about our engagement."

"You want to break it off," she said.

Was that disappointment I heard in her voice? I wished I could see her expression.

"That's not what I want," I said hastily.

"Then what do you want?"

"I want to make it real."

I saw the shock on her face as a car backfired. The noise was enough to startle the horses.

As I tried to calm my horse, Rowan's horse bucked and galloped away. She cried out in surprise as the horse charged down the track. I set off in pursuit, praying her bay mare would have enough sense not to head out of the gate at the end of the track. I could see Rowan hanging on for dear life.

I might have been able to reach her and calm the mare if the second backfire hadn't echoed around the estate. The horse panicked again, and I watched in horror as the woman I loved was thrown off, landing heavily on the hard ground.

Chapter 23

Rowan

Adam drove the Land Rover as close to the side door of the house as he could, so I didn't have to walk too far. I'd been so lucky. Adam had insisted on driving me to the hospital. My left ankle was sprained but not badly. Apart from a few bruises and the sprain I was fine. I'd been more concerned about the horses, but fortunately, they were unharmed.

"Thanks," I said and opened the car door.

He sighed, unhappy that I'd refused his offer of help into the house. "You don't have to run away."

"I don't think I'll be running anywhere," I quipped. I smiled, but Adam didn't return it.

I bit my bottom lip. "I'm not running from you, Adam. My leg hurts and I just want to put my feet up and think for a while."

"I didn't mean to put pressure on you."

"You didn't. We didn't have time to talk about it before I fell off the horse."

Adam didn't look convinced, but I patted his hand. "We'll talk. Just not now. I need to sleep and think beyond how much my leg hurts."

Most days, I'd invite him in for dinner, but now I just wanted to go hide.

"I'm sorry," he said, and I saw the hurt in his

eyes. But as usual, his first concern was for me. "You're right. I wasn't thinking. You rest and I'll talk to you in the morning."

I took a chance and leaned over to kiss Adam's cheek. "Good night."

He smiled at me and if it wasn't his usual beaming smile, it was good enough. "Sleep tight. Do you need a hand with the steps?"

"I can manage." I assured him.

I was aware of his eyes on me as I limped up the stairs. I should have swallowed my pride and asked for his help.

Of course I had to be caught sneaking back into the house by Harry.

"Why are you limping, dear girl," he called from the doorway of his study. I could hear sounds of gunfire from his videogame.

I stopped to smile at him, shifting my weight off my left leg so it didn't look as if I were in agony. "I took a tumble off a horse."

Harry tsked. "Why didn't Adam bring you back here?"

"He did. And he took me to the minor injuries clinic at the hospital too. It's just a slight sprain, Harry. Nothing serious. I've just got to keep my weight off it for a few days." I smiled at him, not wanting him to worry.

He nodded, although he didn't look convinced. "Could we talk? Just for a few minutes."

I held back a groan because I just wanted to lie down, but Harry had shown me nothing but kindness, so I smiled. "Of course."

Harry strode over to me and offered his arm.

"Let's sit in your study. You can rest your leg on one of the footstalls."

Our progress was slow, but he didn't rush me, and eventually I settled in one of the wingback chairs, my foot resting on a cushion on the footstall. Harry wouldn't talk until I'd had coffee, and in his words, 'stopped looking like a ghost'.

I looked up at him and took a deep breath. "Ready to talk now."

Harry hesitated, but then he nodded. "The family are getting restless, my dear."

The détente with the family had eased the tension. Once they realized I wasn't going to sell the place, disrupt their lifestyles, or scurry away with my tail between my legs, they backed off. But they wanted an answer as much as Adam did.

I gave him an apologetic smile. "I know. I just needed time to think. But I think last week in London consolidated my decision. If my aunts and uncles will support me, I want to take my place here."

"I know we didn't make it easy for you when you arrived, but over the past two months you've proved yourself to be a real Mayfield."

I knew he meant that as the highest compliment, although I'm not sure I took it as such.

"Who looked after Mayfield when Grandfather traveled?" I asked.

Harry looked surprised. "Willow did. She's the only one with any real interest in running the place. You probably know that from talking to the workers on the estate."

I did. Most of them had a lot of time for Willow, even if she was prickly.

"If I stayed here, I'd need to travel."

"I understand," Harry said. "You'll have family business commitments."

I'd been thinking more about my friendship with Lily and Elle. They lived thousands of miles apart. I could fly to see them. But yes, I would have other business commitments and the issue of residency until the visa was sorted.

"Would the family take over when I'm away?" I asked.

Harry inclined his head. "We'd be honored to, my dear."

At least that was one thing off my checklist. If I stayed. Then I shook my head. "Harry, I can't run the estate by myself."

Harry smiled gently at me. "That's why you've got a family to help you."

I stared at him for a moment. I took a deep breath and returned his smile. "Maybe we ought to have a family meeting."

"I think that would be a very good idea." He studied me for a long moment. "Does that mean you're staying?" And I could see the hope in his eyes.

"Do you want me to stay?" I asked.

"Now you've taken time to get to know us, I do. I think you'll be good for us. We can get a bit stuffy."

He wrinkled his nose and I laughed.

"What about Willow and the others?"

"They just want Mayfield to survive," Harry

said.

I thought about it for a moment. Two months ago, I couldn't have cared less. My time away made me realize I did care. And I'd promised Adam I would be by his side.

I grimaced as I knocked my ankle. "I'm going to bed."

Harry leaned forward. "What about Adam? Would you stay for him?"

"He asked me to stay here," I admitted.

A broad smile crossed his face, emphasizing the laughter lines around his eyes. "Good lad. I thought he'd never get around to it."

"He asked me to stay, not marry him," I protested.

"One step at a time, dear girl."

I realize he thought I was grumbling that Adam hadn't proposed. I went to explain but Harry said, "I'll help you up the stairs."

Each step on my sprained ankle was a spike of pain through my body. "I wish you had an elevator," I gasped as we climbed the stairs.

"Lean on me," Harry said. "I asked for one for years, but Father disapproved of anything that didn't fit in keeping with the era."

"Maybe we can find a place out of the way," I suggested.

"You'd have to get the family to agree, but my knees would thank you."

I grinned at Harry. "I can do that."

"I'm sure you can, my dear. I have every faith in you."

He helped me to my bedroom door. I gave him

a hug which seemed to please him. Then I went in and shut the door behind me with a sigh of relief.

I needed time by myself to think.

Just before dawn, I gave up trying to sleep and dressed, limping down the stairs. I ached too much from my fall to stay in bed. It was too early for most of the household, and I knew I'd get a chance to think alone. Normally I'd go for a walk to clear my head, but my ankle wasn't up to any strenuous exercise. Instead I headed to the one place which epitomized my relationship with the Mayfield family—the balcony. Via the kitchen to get coffee of course because I couldn't think without caffeine.

I walked out onto the patio and shivered. Dawn was colder than I expected. I put my coffee on the table and retreated inside to grab the ancient Afghan carefully arranged over the couch. I threw it over my shoulders and returned to the balcony, inhaling the crisp early morning air. It was so clear compared to back home.

Fall was almost over. It was hard to believe my first visit was two months ago. I settled on the balcony and looked out over the endless lawn and formal gardens. I sipped at the hot, strong coffee, welcoming the heat burn through my system.

The sky was the deep indigo blue before dawn. Sunrise wasn't far away. I thought about the sunset Adam and I had shared at Lavender Cottage. Maybe I needed to take time to share many more sunrises and sunsets with him.

"Well, Mom. What do you think? Are you and

Gran happy to see me here?"

Mom didn't answer, which was a relief. I didn't want anyone to catch me talking to myself. They thought I was weird enough as it was.

Truth was, I loved it here. In the two months since my unwelcome arrival something had changed. I'd gotten to know the estate and its people. But it was more than that. Something about this place had gotten under my skin. I watched the sky lighten, bathing the garden with mauves and pinks. It was beautiful here. And it was mine.

If I stayed—and that was a big if—I'd be taking on a huge responsibility. If I didn't stay, I'd be leaving behind my heart.

And there it was. What this whole dawn freak-out was about. It wasn't about being the head of the Mayfield family. I'd made that decision in Boston. It was about offering my heart to the gardener.

I stared down at the half-drunk cup of coffee. "I don't know."

"Know what?" Adam asked.

Of course he had to catch me. I looked down to see him grinning up at me.

"Anything," I admitted. "Anything at all."

He tipped back the ugly hat so he could see me better. "You're up early."

"I needed to think. I didn't really sleep."

Adam nodded. "This time of day is always good for thinking. Want to join me?"

"My ankle hurts," I confessed.

He held out his arms. "I'll carry you."

"You want me to throw myself off the balcony into your arms again?"

It was a joke and Adam waggled his arms. "You know you want to."

He was right of course. I did want to and this time I knew he'd catch me.

The sun was just peeking over the tops of the trees. A new day. A new beginning. It was fitting.

I put down the cup and nodded. "As long as there's coffee."

"There's always coffee," Adam scoffed.

I launched myself into his arms. He caught me easily and held me to his chest.

"We're starting to make a habit of this," I said somewhat breathlessly, smiling at him.

"I hope we'll do it until we're old and gray," he said.

Our gazes locked and I knew what he was asking me. Did I want to stay here to be with him forever?

I looked into his eyes and gave him the only answer I could. "I love you."

Chapter 24

Adam

"You do? You mean that, Rowan Mayfield?"

Rowan nodded and I swung her around until she squealed. "I'm going to throw up. My ankle, my ankle."

I slowed down and held her close. "Thank you," I whispered. "Thank you. I love you too."

She pulled back to look at me. Then had to puff at her hair which had gotten in her eyes. I pushed it back. "Thanks."

"You're welcome."

"You can put me down," Rowan said.

"Knowing you, you'd fall over and break your leg," I grumbled.

She spluttered in indignation, but then she sobered and fixed me with her soft brown gaze. "Adam, I'm here for you and your family. You won't be thrown out of the cottage. And I'll take care of you...when you need me to."

I knew what she was trying to say. She would be here for me and Mom when we needed it most. I held her close again. "Thank you. I wish I could have been there for you when you lost your mom."

She sighed and put her head on my shoulder. "It was so hard," she admitted. "It was just her and me, even at the funeral."

My heart ached for her. Her family could have made so much difference just by one call, yet they left her alone. She must find it hard not to be resentful.

Rowan smiled at me. "It's okay, Adam. I loved my mom. All we needed was each other."

I kissed her cheek.

"Where are we going?" she asked as I set off down the path.

"My shed," I said. "I have coffee."

"What time did you start work?"

"Five as usual."

"You've been getting up at five every day just so you could spend time with me and your dad, haven't you?"

I hesitated, then said, "I get up early anyway. It was no big deal. Charlie's a great boss, but he gets annoyed if we don't make up our hours."

"You should have told me," she murmured. "What about the week we were away?"

"I had vacation due."

"You used your vacation week to take care of me?"

"I went in a private jet to Boston and a beach cottage in Maine," I pointed out with a broad grin. "It wasn't a hardship."

We'd reached the shed. I nudged open the door, smelling the aroma of freshly brewed coffee. I placed Rowan on the seat and propped her injured ankle on a wooden crate covered with a towel.

"Thanks. I never thought a sprained ankle

could be this painful." But she managed to grin at me as I rolled my shoulders. "How's your back feeling now?"

I groaned and hammed it up. "I've been feeding you too much."

"Poor baby," she cooed. "But isn't it me feeding you?"

"Is that sarcasm I hear?"

"Never," she declared and then smirked.

I shook my head as I poured out the dark brew and gave her a cup. "Don't ever change, Rowan Mayfield."

"I can promise you that won't happen," she assured me.

I perched on the desk and looked down at her. "How do you think the family will take it?"

Rowan nodded, nibbled on her bottom lip, and said, "Uncle Harry spoke to me last night. I think they'll be fine. They just needed my commitment."

"What did you tell him?"

"I said I couldn't look after the estate by myself." She gave me a wry smile. "He said that's what family was for. I've never had a family like this. It will take time."

"They know that. They've never had anyone like you before. I think you'll be good for each other."

But Rowan carried on. She had something to get off her chest. "I want to travel. To do things I couldn't do before. I promised Davy a donation for the animal sanctuary. Mr. Roberts says the visa is progressing. He hinted that marriage would help my chances. But traveling to Boston will give me a chance to meet up with Elle and Lily."

"Will you buy the condo?"

She hesitated. "Maybe. It's not vacant yet."

"And it's a lot of money."

"So much money," she agreed. "Lily has given me another option. She might buy it and rent it to me."

I knew Lily would do that in a heartbeat if it made Rowan more comfortable. "I really like her."

"Me too," Rowan agreed. "I'm so grateful for our friends. They understand me. And Willow used to take care of the estate for William when he was away on business. Harry says the family will do the same for me."

"Sounds like you've thought this through," I said.

"Yes, and no." Rowan huffed out a breath. "I don't think I've stopped thinking since I knew I wanted to stay here...with you."

My heart flip-flopped at her honest admission. Me. Not Mayfield.

Rowan looked at me. "I need to talk with all my family. But I need to know what you'll do. I know your Mom wants to go back to Boston. Will you go with her?"

"I've been thinking about that too. Mom and I talked about it. I don't think Mom will rush back to Boston. She's made a lot of friends here and she'd just gotten permission to work when Dad got sick. Do you think we could find her a job on the estate so she could keep the cottage?"

Rowan nodded. "Of course, we can find a job

for her. But the cottage is hers for as long as she wants it. And she could stay in the condo if she wanted to visit Boston."

I grinned at the thought of my mom staying in a condo. She'd be afraid to touch anything.

"I know Harry would be gutted if she left," Rowan said." And Charlie too."

"Charlie would miss her cakes," I said and she laughed.

"I've never met a man so addicted to baking. But you haven't really answered my question."

"I want to be with you, Rowan." I assured her.

"You do?"

"I do." It sounded like a vow and maybe it was time to make a proper one. I fumbled in my pocket for the small box I'd been carrying around for weeks. Rowan's eyes went comically wide when I opened my palm. "Adam?"

I knelt beside the chair. "We've got an entire estate. I was going to do this somewhere more romantic than my dad's old shed, but I want you to know I've been thinking about this as much as you have." I flipped open the box to show the square-cut sapphire. "I want to make our fake engagement a real one. Rowan, I don't want you just to stay with me. Would you marry me and throw yourself off the balcony into my arms forever?" My hands shook as I took the ring out of the box and held it out to her.

"Yes. I will, Adam." Rowan's hands shook as much as mine.

I felt as if I didn't breathe until I heard her say yes. I slipped the ring on her finger. It fitted as if it were made for her. "This was my grandmother's engagement ring. My dad's mom. I can get a new ring if you'd prefer," I added hastily. "Although I gotta confess, I don't have the money to buy a ring yet."

Rowan covered her finger as if she were worried I'd snatch it away. "This means more to me than any ring from a store." She stared at it for a long time. "It's so beautiful. Are you sure your dad would be okay about this?"

"Dad insisted. She had her wedding ring, and an eternity ring Dad wants to see worn by the right girl. That's you," I added hastily in case there was any doubt.

"He's so kind." Rowan stroked the sapphire.

"Dad likes you. Which is more than I can say for some of the other girls I brought home."

Rowan side-eyed me. "Should I be worried about these other girls?"

"No. None of them compare to you," I assured her.

"Good answer." At my loud sigh of relief, Rowan's lips twitched, then she giggled. "You should see your face. Don't worry. I'm not going to interrogate you about past relationships."

"There weren't many," I said. "I've been too busy to get involved. What about you?"

Rowan shook her head. "No one really. One or two high school crushes, but I was always the weird kid, you know? The jocks weren't interested in me, and the nerds and geeks were more interested in whatever they were nerding and geeking about."

I picked up her hand and pressed a kiss to her palm. "It's you and me forever, kid."

Her smile was sweet. "I can live with that. Now I think we ought to tell your parents."

I groaned. "You know Mom's gonna want to plan the wedding."

Her eyes lit up. "Really?"

"No, no, no. This is my mom. It's a really bad idea."

Rowan fixed me with a firm look. "Adam Carless, what do you know about organizing a wedding in England?"

"Uh...nothing."

She could have stopped after wedding. I knew nothing about weddings. I'd only been invited to Greg and Lily's wedding, and I hadn't been able to go because Dad had taken a turn for the worse and I couldn't leave my mom.

"Which is about as much as I do. So your mom can plan away." Her expression softened. "Let her do this. She needs something else to think about."

Her thoughtfulness took my breath away. "What about your family. Won't they want to be involved?"

"If Aunt Willow plans the wedding, we won't know a single guest and it will be in British newspapers. We'll probably get a magazine deal too."

"That sounds horrific." I shuddered at the thought. "My mom it is."

"If she wants to," Rowan warned, but I knew my mom. She would be thrilled at the idea.

Rowan picked up her cup, took a sip, and

grimaced. "It's cold."

The coffee had been forgotten in the excitement and confessions. "Let's go and tell Mom and Dad. We can drink their coffee instead," I suggested.

I hauled Rowan gently to her feet and raised an eyebrow. "Want me to carry you again?"

She grimaced. "I didn't realize a sprained ankle could be this painful."

"Is that a yes?"

"Let me lean on you instead. I don't want to break your back."

"Sweetheart, I'm twice your size. I think I can carry you to the car." I thought she'd come back with a quip. Instead she nodded. Rowan had to be in pain. I picked her up and she wrapped her arms around my neck.

"Aren't you supposed to be resting your ankle today?" I asked as we walked to the car.

"I have been resting it," she pointed out. "I was sitting on the balcony. Then you carried me and put my foot on the crate. The only thing I did was walk downstairs."

"You need to get an elevator installed."

Rowan laughed. "That's what Uncle Harry said. Where's the Honda?"

"Mom needs it. Charlie said I could borrow the Land Rover for the day."

"We need to get you your own vehicle," she muttered, almost under her breath, as she climbed in the vehicle, hissing as she put weight on her bad ankle.

I was about to protest. I didn't need her buying

me a truck. Then I thought about it for a moment. If I was going to be the husband to the head of the Mayfield family, I had to make compromises too. "Rowan, if you become the head of the family, what does that make me?"

She looked startled. "I guess I still thought you'd be the gardener. It's what you love."

I breathed a sigh of relief. Rowan didn't expect me to do nothing.

"What do you want to do?" she asked. "I assume you're not taking Greg's offer."

"Not if I stay with you. I want to keep working in the garden, but maybe..." I trailed off because I'd asked before and always been flatly rejected by Charlie who said there was no budget. "I need an assistant. I have a team, but I need someone to manage things when I'm not here."

Rowan nodded. "Especially if you'll be traveling with me."

I hadn't thought about that, but yes. I wouldn't be happy with her leaving me for months to return to Boston.

"I'll talk to Charlie and Willow," she said.

Maybe there could be advantages to loving the woman in charge. I drove out of the gate with a smile on my face.

Epilogue

Rowan

I married my love in the chapel on the estate nearly five months after I arrived in England, on a bright and crisp, if bitterly cold, Christmas Eve. We would have delayed the wedding until the summer, but Adam's dad wanted to see him married and we knew he didn't have long. He couldn't leave his bed, but I drove over before the wedding to show him my dress. Charlie had picked Adam and Greg up and they were doing some guy thing before the ceremony. Adam didn't have a clue what it was, but he said Charlie was insistent.

Allyson fussed over me when I arrived, but I could see she was thrilled I'd made the effort.

"He's tired," she warned.

"We won't stay long."

Simon's face lit up when he saw me walk in with my bouquet of white and red roses. My dress was a simple silk shift with a sweetheart neckline, made by Greg's sister, Valerie. Because of the cold I wore a warm velvet cape and a hat to match. For now, I wore soft, calf-length, red boots which I'd change when I got to the chapel.

"You look beautiful, Rowan," Simon husked.

I smiled at my future father-in-law. I noticed

he'd been shaved, and Allyson had pinned a boutonniere of white and red roses to his pajamas. "You look very smart today."

"I've got to make the effort for my boy and his lovely bride."

But I could see how tired he looked. I leaned over to kiss him on the cheek. "We'll be back later, I promise."

"You enjoy your day and don't worry about an old man."

I blinked back tears because Simon was only in his late fifties, but the cancer had worn him down, body and soul.

Allyson hugged me tight, but careful not to crush my dress. "I'll see you at the chapel."

I was surprised she wasn't already there as she was the planner, but of course, Simon was her priority.

"Barry's going to take me on a tour of the surrounding villages," I said.

"Don't be late," she warned.

"We won't."

I'd been thrilled when I'd walked down the steps of the house, to discover Willow and Ash hovering in front of the Mustang, decorated with a white ribbon on the hood.

"You needed something from home," Ash said brusquely, and told me to stop fussing when I hugged her. But she was pleased, I could see that.

I was even more thrilled to discover Barry was my chauffeur, dressed up in a smart suit and a cap.

I arched an eyebrow. "You flipped a coin with

Alfie?"

"I won." He gave me an awkward bow, then hugged me gently when I held out my arms.

As we drove through the villages, I learned more about the history of the surrounding area. It turned out Barry was something of a local history expert.

"I hope I'm not boring you, Rowan," he asked, partway through a discussion on the Georgian influence on a pub.

"Not at all," I said honestly.

"Good. Because everyone else tells me to shut up. Especially Alfie. I think they might have heard it once or twice before."

Finally though, Barry said, "We should go to the chapel."

I took a deep breath. "Let's do it."

He gave me a quick glance. "Are you nervous?"

"You have no idea."

"You'll be just fine," Barry assured me.

It was kind of him to try to calm me, even though I was ready to leap out of my skin.

All too soon we were outside the chapel.

"Leave the engine running, Barry, in case either of us needs to run," I ordered.

Barry chuckled. "Adam said you'd say that. He told me to tell you he loves you and can't wait to be your husband."

I couldn't even panic without him thinking of me.

"I can do this," I muttered.

"He also said the sooner you get in there, the sooner you can have coffee."

I wrinkled my nose. "He knows me far too well."

"Go on," Barry urged. "He might need you right now."

I was out of the car like a shot. What was wrong? Why hadn't Adam called me?

"Rowan! Wait! Your shoes!" Barry called.

But I didn't stop, too worried about Adam. I ran in the door. Harry waited for me in the porch, dressed in a charcoal-gray Italian wool suit. His tie had discreet red and white roses on them as did all the men in the wedding party. He was going to walk me down the aisle.

"Where's Adam? Is he all right?"

Harry furrowed his brow. "He's fine. Waiting for you with Greg."

I looked and there he was, laughing with Greg. What was Barry talking about?

"I just thought...no, I'm fine." I inhaled and exhaled, then smiled at Harry. "Let's get in there. It's cold out here."

I tucked my hand in the crook of his elbow and put a smile on my face. Then I stopped. "Are you sure Adam's okay, Uncle Harry. He's not just faking it, is he?"

Harry blinked, then patted my hand. "It's the first time you've called me Uncle. Adam is fine. What made you think he's not?"

"Barry said he might need me."

"Of course he needs you. That's why you're getting married," Harry said soothingly.

It was only as the doors opened and the music started, I realized he hadn't really answered the question. But then Adam turned and saw me, and at his broad smile, any worries flew out of my mind. Here was my husband-to-be. Greg had taken him out to buy a suit and he looked incredible.

I walked down the aisle, smiling at Elle and Davy and Lily who sat on the groom's side, and my family who sat on mine. Then I noticed a space where Allyson should be. Maybe Simon had taken a turn for the worse after I'd left.

Greg winked at me, then Adam smiled as I reached him. "You look stunning."

"So do you. Are you all right?" I searched his face anxiously for anything I'd missed. "Your mom—"

"She said she'll be five minutes late."

That was a relief. I didn't want her to miss the wedding she'd arranged.

The vicar of the parish church smiled at us. "Rowan and Adam, it's so good to see you here today with all your family and friends. Well, not quite all." He looked to the side doors and nodded. Two men opened them, and Allyson walked in, in front of a hospital bed.

"Dad." Adam sounded choked up.

Now it made sense. Of course he needed me.

"Go hug him," I urged.

Adam rushed over and hugged his dad, who was now in a jacket and shirt, with the same silk tie as the wedding party. He was also smothered in blankets.

"Can't stay for long, so get on with it, boy," Simon grumbled. He looked exhausted, so I tugged Adam back to the priest.

I can't say I remember much of the wedding ceremony, but Adam hung onto my hand, and I didn't let it go.

Simon needed to go home straight after the service, but the photographer took a photo of him and Allyson with Adam and I, then he left. Adam went with him to the private ambulance as I discovered.

"Who arranged that?" I asked Allyson.

"Your family." She nodded over to Willow and Ash. "They've arranged for two nurses to be with him all day. They insisted Simon didn't miss the ceremony."

I stalked over to my aunts and hauled them into my arms for a fierce hug. "Thank you, Aunt Willow, Aunt Ash. I won't forget this."

"It's the least we could do," Ash muttered. "Put me down, girl."

But I hugged them one more time before I let go and I swear I heard a sob from Willow when I called her aunt again.

It was too cold to take more than one or two photos outside, so we retired to the house.

I hugged Elle and Lily. "Thank you for coming all this way."

Elle was dressed in a blue silk dress, and Lily in a lavender suit. Davy, Greg, and Adam were in deep conversation.

"We wouldn't have missed this for the world," Lily assured me. "Besides, I get to see Greg in a suit, and it doesn't happen nearly enough."

Elle gave a wry smile. "There was no way I was

going to get Davy in a suit."

Her husband was a farmer. He wore a jacket and designer denim. It was a compromise that worked for them both.

"Where's little Skip?" I asked Elle.

"He's at home with Aunty Robyn and Uncle Griff. He's a menace. I didn't think you'd appreciate him screaming up and down the aisle."

"He's welcome here any time," I assured her.

Adam wrapped me in his arms. "Who's welcome here?"

"Baby Skip," I said.

Adam nodded. "Of course he is. And so is your baby, Lily."

My jaw dropped open. "You're having a baby?"

She stared at him. "Greg told you."

Now Adam looked confused. "He told us just now."

Elle didn't look surprised, so she obviously knew.

Lily huffed out a breath. "We were keeping it quiet until after the first trimester."

"But everything is all right?" I asked.

"My little girl is fine," Lily said, placing her hand on her belly.

"You're having a daughter?" I blinked away sudden tears.

"We are. In the early summer." Lily's smile lit up the room.

"Congratulations."

Lily hugged me. "This is meant to be about you two, not us. You're Mr. and Mrs. Carless. Or are you keeping the Mayfield name?"

"No, I'm going to be Rowan Carless."

Adam and I had talked about it, but I wanted to take his name. I would keep Mayfield as a middle name.

Elle and Lily had both taken their husband's names, to some family resistance. I'd politely told my family to get over it. I was a married woman now. Besides there was precedence. I remembered the stories Uncle Raymond told me.

Then Lily and Elle were captured by their husbands, and I turned to face Adam.

"Can you hold me for a while?"

He tugged me in close and enfolded me in his arms. "It's been an intense day."

I rested my head on his chest. "It's been perfect. But I don't want to go through it again."

"Once is enough. Besides, I'm not letting you marry anyone else." Adam stroked my hair. "Do you think your mom would have liked today."

"She'd have hated it," I admitted. "She hated any attention. But she would have loved you and that's all that matters."

"I can't believe Dad was there."

I looked up at him and cupped his jaw. "We should check on him soon."

"We're supposed to be here for our guests," he pointed out.

"Our family is more important. Besides, look at them. They're all fine."

And they were. Ash and Willow acted as hosts. Uncle Harry looked after everyone. Raymond was talking to a man I recognized from working on the estate. They didn't need us for a while. So we bundled up in coats and hats and gloves, and walked toward his parents' cottage.

"I can't wait to get back to Lavender Cottage," Adam said. "We'll watch the sunset again. It was magical."

We would return for our honeymoon, but not while his parents needed him.

"It was magical because you were there," I told him.

Adam's smile was sweet. "Is that a snowflake on your nose?"

"I thought it was meant to rain," I said.

I wanted to capture the joy on Adam's face as he looked up into the snow-filled sky.

"Maybe it's magical just for us." Adam held my hands against his heart and pressed a tender kiss to my lips. "Aren't we lucky?"

I kissed him again as huge snowflakes settled around us. "Yes, we are."

Also by Emma Lewis.

You can find all of Emma's books over at Amazon. Don't forget to sign up for her newsletter.

https://landing.mailerlite.com/webforms/landing/u4n6w6?

About Emma Lewis

Emma is new to this genre, but not to writing romance. It's her joy to make two people live happily ever after. She hopes one day it will happen to her, but in the meantime, she shares her life with her dog and her collection of arc deco lamps.

Come over and talk to Emma at:
Newsletter:
https://landing.mailerlite.com/webforms/landing/u4n6w6?
Website: https://emmalewisromance.com/
Bookbub:
https://www.bookbub.com/profile/emma-lewis
Author group – Facebook:
https://www.facebook.com/groups/394860531894731
Facebook:
https://www.facebook.com/emmalewisromance/
Twitter: https://twitter.com/EmmaLewisBooks
Email: emmalewisromance@gmail.com